Revenge on the Mountain

By

Mark A. Herbkersman

Pete!
Enjoy the journey
Mark

This is a work of fiction. Any connection of the names in this novel to people in real life is very much coincidental.

Check out these other titles in the Henry Family Chronicles:

Book 1: Prodigal's Blood

Book 3: The Branding of Otis Henry (Available autumn 2015)

The book cover is designed by Jeffrey S. Dowers, a dear friend with a talent beyond my own.

Author's notes

The incidents in this story are roughly placed in the Bitterroot Range of Idaho, perhaps more specifically in the Lemhi Range. Of course, as most authors, I have taken liberties with reality to allow for the needs of the story.

I used to do some backpacking in Idaho in my high school and post high school years. We were a bit foolish perhaps, but the trips made for memories that last till today.

I give thanks for those who helped make this book more than a dream. Joni and Kay, my thanks cannot be measured for your help in editing and revising.

To Jeff: thanks for our reawakened friendship.

To my daughters, who witnessed too many times my tendency to be preoccupied and talk about my books too much.

To my wife, Marilyn, who deserves much credit for putting up with me while I wrote.

Foremost, I must acknowledge that God has blessed me with a Lord and Savior as well as creativity and a desire to write. May His will be done.

Chapter 1

"Daddy!"

Lemuel Teague awoke in a sweat, gasping for breath, the voice in the dream as real and tangible as the saddle under his head and the sounds of the night. The visions, the sound...

He groaned, the sound deep and desperate, and lay looking at the millions of stars covering the clear moonless night in the mountain valley.

He would never forget the day of the bank robbery, hearing the shooting, running to the scene, arriving to find the constables running to the bank. There was a shout.

"They've gone out the back!"

"Garner! Get our horses and bring them here, quick!"

The constable had cautiously approached the entrance, until they heard the scream of a teller inside the bank.

"Help! He shot them!"

Along with the constable, he had run into the bank and desperately looked around. His wife and son lay in a corner with the teller kneeling beside them. He knelt in panic, head turning from one to the other. His eight-year old son screamed to him as he lay writhing in the last pain before lapsing into an unconsciousness from which he'd never returned. Tears coursed his face as he turned to his wife and gathered her in his arms. Her eyes looked at him dimly as the red stain spread.

"Anna! Hang on. Don't leave me!"

People had gathered around as the doctor hurried in with his case and knelt beside Jimmy.

Anna's eyes turned to his. "Jimmy?" Her voice was barely a whisper.

He had looked over at the Doctor, meeting the man's eyes, which had a look of resignation as the man pursed his lips tightly.

Teague had turned to his wife, looked down in her eyes and she, even in her last moments, read his grief and knew. The little light left in her eyes vanished and her body slowly relaxed as she died.

No one involved that day would forget the scream that erupted from the throat of Lemuel Teague as his world collapsed and darkness fell like a veil over his heart. Being a minister of a local church there in St Louis, he was respected and listened to and sought for his skills at bringing understanding of the Word of God. His gentleness and warm smile were known throughout the town. They had lived a blissful existence.

All of that life shattered into a million pieces that day.

The men had never been found, and the descriptions were vague. Only a brief word that one man had a birthmark over his left eye.

For four years the cry of his son and the fading light in his wife's eyes had haunted him every night, and he awoke each night in a panicky, suffocating sweat, his lungs heaving and his heart racing. Then came the tears, though not as overwhelming as they once were – especially at first.

He lay awake listening to the night sounds as his heart slowly eased its pounding and his breathing became less consuming. He threw off his blanket to dry his sweat-soaked shirt.

Maybe he needed to find a town, to get away from this solitude that seemed to draw his thoughts to an inescapable past and the terrifying memories of the end of a happy life that was once his. He needed to get away from memories, if only for a brief time.

Besides, after a month in the mountains, he had a hankering for a few words, even if they were only, "rye," and, "where's the best place for a man to bed down?"

At dusk two days later he had topped a rise and seen an unexpected twinkle of lights and decided a drink and a bed might be his tonight.

Tuned acutely to his surroundings, he took in the moonlit countryside as he approached. He noted draws, copses of trees and finally the layout of buildings. Quick glances were all he needed, as his mind instinctively did the rest. It was the way of his life in recent years. He had survived – so far – by keeping aware.

Stopping for a few moments at a point on the trail, he took out a worn bandana and, taking off his spectacles, gave them a good cleaning before replacing them. Satisfied, he walked his horse toward town.

He rode a large horse, noticed by many. At seventeen hands, he attracted stares that were not always welcome, often covetous. The horse was a stunning gray half Arabian cross that was intelligent and strongly connected to its rider. They had traveled many trails together and seemed to anticipate each other. Calm amidst gunfire, the horse – Rex – would stay ground-tied for hours. Teague was a large muscular man and needed a big horse. This one had been given to him over a year ago by his cousin's family out of New Haven, Colorado. He remembered sitting in his Uncle Otis Henry's home, across from his cousins. He had not seen most of them ever before, except for Bill Henry, whom he had known in the East when Bill was a prominent attorney in Boston. He'd made a couple trips to Boston and had made a point of connecting. Then Bill went west again. His kinfolk had welcomed him and done all they could to ease his troubled state of heart. When it was clear he would head west they surprised him with Rex as a gift. The Circle-H brand of Otis Henry daily reminded him of the generosity of his cousins, who themselves had not long before been through a difficult time and fought tenaciously to keep their ranch and their lives.

Looking down at Rex, Lemuel Teague sighed and pulled his gun, spun the cylinder and paused for a brief moment before he replaced it in his holster.

Scores of people attended the funeral of his wife and son. He remembered little, as he was in deep darkness in his heart, his spirit perplexed and agonizing over this tragedy. As he threw the first handfuls of dirt upon the caskets, the hollow sound broke even deeper into his soul, and a deep burning rage filled the new void.

Leaving the funeral, shaking the obligatory hands and hearing too many platitudes, his next stop had been the gunsmith, where he purchased matching .44's and a holster, along with an excessive supply of shells. He had become reclusive, and went each day to a secluded glade in the hills, where he alternately prayed, screamed in anguish, gritted with rage and practiced with his guns.

He heard no answer from God that pleased him, his anger kept him from his Bible, and his natural skill with weapons became unleashed in a lightning draw.

Then came the day when he rode out of town, the darkness and a determination visible to all on his already rapidly changed visage.

Shaking his head, Teague returned to the present. He patted Rex.

"Well, Rex, I reckon you'd like something different to eat, like maybe some oats or corn. I'd like a change of feed myself. Let's mosey in and see what we can find."

Once he had been asked about the horse, "It looks half Arabian – what's the other half?" He had replied, "some lucky stallion that got thru the fence."

As he neared the town, he paused again. He noted how it was the same as so many hundreds of towns around the West, with gray-weathered lumber and crude hitching posts. The first buildings were usually placed so as to form a semblance of a street, but beyond the main street the other buildings were placed haphazardly, wherever the owner had a whim. There was always a saloon, likely the first building raised, followed by a general store, then another saloon, a few cribs for the ladies who seemed to show up eventually to ply the oldest trade, and then a smattering of other establishments. Last but not least there seemed to pop up a sheriff's office as a sort of afterthought to try to quell the tendency of original sin.

This town appeared to be smaller than some, larger than others.

It was said that he often knew what was to happen before it actually came to be. He smiled at the thought...his "foresight" was merely founded on a deep awareness of men, women and his surroundings. He felt that senses needed to be used in proportion to their provision – two ears, two eyes, two nostrils and one mouth. If used this way, a man could perceive and learn many things.

In the past, he had to admit, he used his mouth more than his other senses. It was what had been expected of his position in society.

That had changed as he found the first of the men involved in the robbery. He had wandered nearby territory for three weeks, having only the meager description. One night he had entered a saloon and noticed a man at a corner table, surrounded by the friends that only buying drinks could find. A common enough looking man but with too much money. As he looked over, the man turned and met his eye. Teague saw the large birthmark over one eye.

He had approached the man's table, stopping across the table from the man with the birthmark. He spoke:

"I loved my wife and son and you took them away from me. The man looked up from his cards, and a dawning realization shown in his face. He slowly rose to his feet, cards forgotten on the table.

"Stranger, I don't know what you're talking about."

"My son was eight years old. My wife was one of a kind. So is that birthmark described by the bank teller."

Realization shown on the man's face. He paled. "Mister, I didn't shoot your wife. The boss did 'cause she saw his face. Honest, it weren't me!"

Lemuel Teague paused a moment to absorb what the man said. The man saw this hesitation in his face and reached for his gun. Teague drew and the man lay dead upon the floor.

"God is our refuge and strength, a very present help in trouble," he muttered to himself.

A hardened man, he had an angular jaw, covered with stubble. He was a mite taller than average, stocky and muscular, wide in the shoulder. His clothes were worn and his buckskin jacket darkened with use and age. Everything about him pointed to average, except the guns and the spectacles

No one there that day would forget either the rage or lightning speed of the man who became known as Preacher. Lemuel Teague now had a reputation.

Now his senses told him something was not right here in this hamlet. Too quiet. Too few horses at the hitching posts for a place this size. A livery stable, bank, two stores, three saloons, what looked like an eating establishment of some kind, a hotel, a few indiscriminate places and a few homes scattered around. His eyes and understanding read the clues in mere moments, as was common to many in the West.

Just a few horses at one saloon. The others seemed to be closed down. Early. A western town should be fully awake about now, with cowhands blowing off steam, townsfolk talking and enjoying the cooler night air, perhaps the strains of a tinpanny piano drifting in the breeze. Nothing.

The last thing he wanted was to walk into somebody else's trouble again. It seemed to follow him ever since…

After a momentary flickering thought of turning and heading back into the hills, he sighed and headed to the active saloon. He really wanted something to cut the trail dust. Not a stranger to the ways of the west – and still alive – he loosened his gun in its holster.

His guns were well-oiled and cared for. One in the holster and another in his waistband. What many didn't see was a 5-shot 31 caliber "Baby Patterson" behind his left hip. And, behind his gun, an Arkansas toothpick rode against the right hip, razor sharp and ready to hand. Only he knew of a similar knife in his boot – a little extra insurance he had benefitted from in past situations. Another pistol rested in his saddle-bags, next to Plutarch and some writings of John Wesley tucked next to a well-worn Bible. A scabbard hung from his saddle and held a Colt revolving shotgun.

The spectacles were a necessity. He carried a spare set in his saddlebags. The product of that earlier and happier time of life, they were more of a hindrance now, giving him a look that stood out in a crowd. A studious and stern look all at once. Some seemed to interpret the wearing of spectacles as a sign of weakness. When riding the hills, his mind often strayed to those days of a different life, and the contentment that eluded him now. He had bristled at the thought of wearing spectacles, yet his studious life had strained his vision and the traveling eye doctor had readily fit him with what he needed.

Chapter 2

Dismounting at the open saloon, he did not tie Rex, but merely let the reins drop and mounted the steps, pausing to look over the batwings.

A handful of men. No-accounts by their looks. Two were leaning back in their chairs and looking important in the way they blew cigar smoke and talked loud. A bartender was polishing glasses with a wary sense of boredom. Another almost-man stood talking loudly at the bar, with large yellowed gap-teeth, a flattened nose and a wispy wanna-be beard of a kid who needed to prove his importance. Lemuel Teague had seen the look before, and this time it was combined with a face that reminded him of an in-bred mountain boy.

He pushed through the batwings and noted eyes riveted on him with startled anxiety. They must have expected someone else, but they quickly resumed their other activities. The air was tense. He walked to the bar.

"Rye."

Taking his first sip and casually looking in the mirror, he noted the men giving him sideways glances. The wanna-be had gone over to another table and was talking quietly but earnestly with another. It was as if they were trying to decide something. Were they expecting someone else?

"Always this quiet?" He asked the bartender.

A pin dropping would have sounded like an avalanche in the instant silence that filled the room. After a moment, he heard a chair scrape behind him and glancing quickly in the mirror, he saw a lean-jawed man with a self-important air approach and face him. He had the strut of a Banty rooster.

Here we go again, Teague thought to himself. He should have just gone back into the hills and camped. It seemed like he just attracted trouble. Ah, well, he thought. Once it confronted him, he didn't shy away. In fact, as always, a deep anger quickly built up inside him. He resented those who put trouble on him for no reason. He just wanted a drink and a bed. And now this no-account rooster who needed to crow was going to ruin his evening.

"You got a name, mister?" The man asked with a sense of importance.

"Leave me alone." It was said casually with a slight insistence.

The rooster was not to be pushed away so easily.

"Hey, four-eyes. I'm askin' you if you got a name?"

Anger welled up from deep inside as he sipped again. He could not keep it from showing in his voice as he met the man's gaze in the mirror.

"Mister, I came in here off the trail, wanting a drink. I say it again, leave me alone." He bit the words off with emphasis.

The man was wary and shifted his weight, but was too filled with self-importance and rotgut to back off.

"My name is Cletus McNary. We ain't takin' to strangers here. What's your name and what's your business here?"

The others watching later said they had never seen a gun come out so fast. It was a blurr and McNary was bug-eyed as he stared at the cold barrel of a .44.

"I said leave me alone. Go sit down and let me drink."

All eyes stared as one at the stranger and the rage in his eyes.

McNary raised his hands and backed slowly to his chair and sat down. He was not seen by his fellows as a coward, but as a smart man, for a man would be stupid – and dead – to have pushed the issue in the face of that gun barrel, backed by a man with such livid anger in his eyes.

Teague turned back to his drink, laying the gun beside him on the bar, close to hand, and staring deliberately at the rooster as he did so. His anger was deep, his heart pounding, and like other times he could barely control it.

A few minutes later the men carefully got up and walked out the batwings.

Focusing on the bartender, Teague asked, "You seem scared. Of me or those two-bit hirelings?"

"Mister, I gotta be careful what I say. Those men would tear me up if'n they knew I was telling you anything."

"Look down at the bar and clean the glasses. Speak soft and don't look at me. Start with what's the name of this place?"

"West Platte, but some is calling it Bark-ersville."

"Why Barkersville?"

"On account of Big John Barker. He come into the area nigh on to six months ago, him and his men. They done laid claim to almost a hundred square miles of the territory hereabouts. Most everybody's lost most their cattle, disappearing at night."

"Other ranchers stood up to him?"

"He bought them out, or so he says. Rumor has it they was told to leave or die. Brock Mettert of the rocking-M put up a fight, but he was found drygulched in the breaks. Shot in the back. When that happened, some of the others done just left. There's an outfit at the edge of the mountains, the bar-slash, still holding out. Old Soldier and Injun fighter named Grizzard. An' then there's Grace Gruber. Word has it that she's in town tonight at the hotel. Barker is telling her to sign over her deed. They done kilt her pa, but she's co-owner in his will. She's to sign in the morning and leave. She and her kid brother – little Luke."

Teague felt the anger rising again. He despised injustice and hated those who took advantage of women and children. His face turned red as he fought for control.

"What about the sheriff?"

Kerner, the bartender, gave a wry smile. He was a man who could read others well also. He knew this man in front of him could be trusted. "Ain't no law here except Barker. One of his puppets plays sheriff and spends most of his time with his feet on the desk ignoring it all."

"This Grace Gruber must be pretty young. She able to run the place without her pa?"

"She's got spunk, about nineteen, I 'spect. Her pa has raised her knowing all about the ranch. It's not the best spread, but they been slowly building. It could be a fine spread some day – one to be proud of. Barker has run off all her help, or at least they's not here anymore." He gave a knowing glance at Teague.

"Anybody else been trying to defy Barker and straighten things out?"

"A couple have tried. They's buried just out of town. Barker's got the whole place tied up. They's some has sold out to him and inform on anybody that speaks against him. We know who some are, but not all. Everybody's scared. On the other hand, might be surprised what might happen if'n the folks think there's a chance." He gave a knowing look to Teague, who let the comment drop. After all, he was just traveling through.

"How old is the boy?"

"I 'spect Luke would be about six. I hear his ma died of the fever when he was a baby. Grace is like his mom. She stepped in and raised him." He backed away and cleaned glasses as they both heard boot steps approaching on the boardwalk. Teague glanced in the mirror and saw one of the recent men glance in and then walk away.

"What happened to her pa?"

"Gunned down. The sheriff said it was a fair fight." A knowing glance to Teague.

"You know that the town will eventually have to do something. You can't go on letting this man treat you like his slaves, cowering and losing your souls."

"Barker will kill anyone who tries."

"There are things worse than death. Will Shakespeare said 'Cowards die many times before their deaths. The valiant never taste of death but once.'"

Kerner looked at him, eyebrow raised.

"Where's the best place to hole up for the night?"

"Hotel's the only spot, less'n you tip ole Fergy at the livery and he'll let you stay in the haymow."

Tossing the rest of his drink, he walked to the batwing, looked both ways and stepped outside and to the left, letting his eyes adjust to the dark. Too many men died by stepping from a bright lit saloon to a dark street without pausing. A perfect place for a set up, taking advantage of the moment of blindness.

Leading Rex to the livery, the hostler was nowhere to be found, so Teague found a stall, unsaddled and rubbed Rex down, then gave him a bait of grain and hay.

Turning to leave, he sensed rather than saw someone rise up from behind a stall. Ducking the blow, he pulled his gun and swung with the barrel. He heard the man fall with a thud. Not wanting to strike a light and make himself a target, he dragged the man closer to the door where a shaft of moonlight broke free and lit the man's face.

One of the men from the saloon!

What was it? What was it about him that he merely came to town for a drink and a bed and wound up in the middle of a mess? Logically, he should saddle up and leave town quickly. Yet something in him said he could wait till morning, spend the night in a soft bed and then carefully leave. This trouble wasn't his.

Lemuel Teague was a man of conflicting emotions. It hadn't always been this way. Only since...since his life fell apart. He once lived a predictable life, a life where his future was something pleasant and helpful to others and a position respected by many. Yet, in recent years, it seemed that he'd had nothing but trouble followed by trouble. Of course, his spectacles set him apart. They were not unknown, but were something expected of storekeepers and those with their noses in books. To see a man ride into town from the open range, looking like a traveling cowhand, but with spectacles, often resulted in questioning looks and, not infrequently, comments and harassment. These did not go well as, since that day 4 years ago, he'd had a deep anger. It was an anger that went to his core yet was just below the surface. Some saw him as unpleasant, as a man to stay away from. Others seemed to see opportunity to challenge, to test his limits. They found his limits were narrow. Then there were those who looked at him and wondered and turned silent.

There were those in town who now also knew that to prod him was not in their best interests.

He shook his head. At one time, people called him happy and content, and he would laugh and get on his knees to play with any child and was eager to hold new babies. He was sought for company at many occasions and was prominent in the community.

All that was past now. He wanted only solitude and the companionship of his own thoughts. He was a man with a varied mission, yet also lost in a sense.

Crossing the street to the hotel, he went to the counter, startling the night clerk who was asleep in a chair.

"I need a room."

"Yessir. A room is a dollar. Just sign the register."

He looked down, seeing only a couple names. Not very busy. He looked more carefully. Grace Gruber. The girl who was being driven off her ranch. Oh well, not his problem. He just needed a good night's sleep and then he'd be leaving.

He shut the door, placed the lone chair under the knob, and stripped down, hanging his holster on the bedpost and placing the Patterson under his pillow. All done without consciously thinking. Habit. Instinct. The way of a man and the price of survival in the West.

As he drifted between sleep and wakefulness, he saw the face of his wife as the spark of life left her. He sat up, sweating though the night was cool.

It was the same every night, and had been since....He lay back down and tossed in agony. Unable to get the memory to depart. He and Anna had been delightfully happy. She came from Fancy Gap, Virginia. A simple yet refined young lady, with a way about her that endeared her to everybody. They had met when she was visiting Boston. She had not had much, was embarrassed by the fancy dresses of the town. He had seen beyond the clothes to the woman inside. Their courtship had been short, and Jimmy arrived shortly after their first anniversary.

"Daddy!" He grabbed his ears, writhing in the emotional agony that had been a daily burden. They were the voices from within, from the end of happiness. He was a hard man, but tears welled in his eyes, as they did many nights, and he took ragged breaths, seeking to calm himself. He finally drifted into restless sleep.

Chapter 3

Awakening with the dawn, he heard a voice in the hall, apparently talking through a door. The paper-thin walls of such frontier hotels made them barely more private than the outdoors.

"Miss Gruber!" The voice was forceful, haughty. He recognized the voice of the rooster from the saloon.

"Miss Gruber! Mister Barker says it's time. He wants you at the dining room in 15 minutes."

"Tell Big John Barker I will be there when I'm good and ready!" It was a voice both resigned but with defiant sarcasm, he thought. A girl with spunk in the face of what life threw at her. He heard the man's footsteps fade down the hall.

"Better get up, Luke. Time we best get on."

"Why do we have to leave, Grace? Can't we fight?"

"We got no fight left, Luke. They've killed or run off ever-blessed one of the hands."

"What about grandpa?"

"Hush, Luke. Nobody but us knows about that. We ain't going to crawl to nobody."

"Where'r we gonna go, Grace?"

"I don't rightly know, Luke. We'll head west somewhere."

As he lay in his room listening. He felt the anger rise in him again. He was sensitive to injustice, to the workings of men who sought to take from those unable to defend themselves. What was going on here? Who was this Big John Barker who seemed to have the country tied up? What was happening?

The town had most likely started like so many others, with a wagon train headed west. Then, someone either got tired of traveling or a wagon broke down and the town sprung from that. From the looks of the buildings, the town had risen to prosperity, and many had made their homes and futures here. Ranchers had tied up with townsfolk and a flourishing economy had begun. Then, somewhere along the way, a predator had arrived and subtly taken hold. He had seen it before. Some towns seemed able to rise up and overcome, throwing down evil. Others seemed to give in and lose their identity.

He tried in his mind to tell himself that this was not his trouble, but his mind would not let him.

"Look after widows and orphans in their distress." The words flashed in his mind with vibrancy and with the power of his past and the seeming destiny of his life. He had heard the words in his mind many times. He began to sweat again. Who were this Grace and her brother Luke? Were they not widows and orphans? Who were these men who had set him up in the livery stable? Who did his assailant work for? He suspected the employer was this Big John Barker.

He had a deep distaste of anybody who felt compelled to have the name "big" thrown in front of his name. A haughty sense of self-importance. It reminded him of his nemesis on the wagon train west when he was a kid.

"Big Mike" had been the bully of the wagon train kids. He strutted and got his way, by force if necessary. Big Mike was a mirror image of his father who tried to bluster the men of the train. Both the father bear and his cub saw themselves as better and smarter than others. He remembered his own pa telling Big Mike and his pa to take cover as the Indians swarmed the train. The other man had paused to respond sarcastically to the order and the instant of pride brought an arrow to the throat. The son had been killed beside the father.

28

Teague heard the door down the hall open and close and footfalls recede down the steps. A deep resolution mixed with resignation built within him. Arising, he sighed and blew his cheeks, then splashed water on his face and quickly dressed. Hitching his gun belt to settle it on his hips, he carefully opened the door and stepped into the hall.

Of such moments are futures made.

Quietly taking the back stairs, he glanced around the corner to see a man standing behind the curtain to the dining room. It was the inbred creature he'd seen the night before and obviously a guard. Glancing quickly around, Teague coughed lightly, but enough that he knew the guard would hear. Sure enough, he heard careful footsteps come down the hall. The man hesitated when he neared the corner. As his head inched around, his throat was seized in Teague's suppressing grip and almost at the same time a fist turned him limp and unconscious. Careful not to let the man fall, he carefully opened a closet door and set the man inside. As he crept to the guard's former station, he heard voices in the dining room. He was unable to see around the corner without revealing himself to the likelihood of another guard.

"Miss Gruber. I expect you to sign immediately."

"What about our clothes and furniture?"

"Your clothes are already in your wagon, which is rigged and ready for your immediate departure. The furniture....shall we say....is needed for the new occupant."

"One of your thugs?"

"I have men of various skills in my employ."

"And what if I refuse to sign?"

"I don't think you should consider that a valid option." The voice was that of a man used to control. There was a definite warning to the words.

"I'd say you have no respect for a woman, either, Mister Barker. You live your life by threats. Only you went beyond threats when you killed my father."

"You have no proof of that."

"We both know the truth."

"Sign."

He heard a chair creak. She must be rising to sign whatever trumped up papers had been prepared. What kind of a show was this? In the West pains were taken not to bother women, but whoever this was didn't let femininity stop his plans.

"I think you have made a wise decision, Miss Gruber. Here is the pen."

Teague stepped out from behind the curtain quickly, taking in the set up before him. At a table sat a man in a fastidious suit, held open by hands held commandingly at the hips. This must be Big John Barker. He was imposing, a bit heavy with a large and carefully trimmed mutton chop beard, narrow eyes and thin-pursed lips.

The young lady stood and her brother was seated in a chair opposite the man. Behind the man stood McNary – the rooster from the saloon, and another man stood by the other door. All looked suddenly at him as he stepped into the room. Another man sat casually off to the side.

"Don't sign it, Miss Gruber."

She paused, looking at the stranger with the stubble and spectacles.

The man in the suit appeared angered.

"Whoever you are, you need to mind your own business and leave! Miss Gruber! Sign the paper – now!"

"Don't sign it!"

"McNary! Where's Johnson? He was supposed to be in the back hallway."

"I dunno, boss."

The man sitting nearby arose slowly, showing his tied-down guns and a crisp appearance. He looked at Teague, his brow wrinkled, as with revelation and excitement. It was the look of a lion facing another, aware of the danger but filled with the excitement of possible conquest. Keeping his hands carefully tucked in his belt, the man spoke, rolling a wheat straw in his teeth.

"Mr. Barker, it's Preacher."

"Carson, I don't care if he's the Pope! Get that misguided parson out of here! Johnson!" He looked to the back entrance where Teague had entered.

The other lion with the wheat straw spoke again, more deliberately. "Mr. Barker...Preacher Teague."

Preacher Teague! The name took assurance away from even the most confident gunmen. The name of a man known for a lightning-quick draw and a rage that erupted and turned him into a driven man. Though he never claimed any, it was rumored that his guns had ended the careers of many men on the dark side of the law. Not a lawman, "Preacher" as he was known, took the side of the downtrodden and oppressed.

The man straightened, all anger suppressed with realization. Preacher! He recovered quickly and spoke off-handed.

"Mr. Teague. I do believe that I am merely concluding a business transaction with this young lady, and I do not believe that your opinion has been requested by either myself or Miss Gruber."

Teague noted Barker making a slight signal to the guard at the door, who suddenly stepped out into the front hallway. The door to the hotel could be heard to open and close. No doubt there would be reinforcements on the way soon.

Miss Gruber had put the pen back down, obviously angering Big John Barker. However, the man calmed and assumed a pandering smile.

"Mr. Teague. It is quite clear that you are a man of accomplishment. You are a man with deep knowledge of the world in which we live. You have a reputation that precedes you. You must understand that this world is filled with two types of people – the have's and the never going to have's. There are many who have but are unable to hold….through a lack of some sort. Then there are the have's, people like me who come along to tame the land and by virtue of natural ability collect the fat of the land unto themselves. And then I employ others, providing a livelihood."

Keeping tuned to noises in the hallway, Teague approached the young lady, who was slender and ladylike. The boy, Luke, stood by, staring up at him. Keeping his hand near his gun, he circled to the table.

"Miss Gruber, are you selling because you want to or because you have been told to?"

"I have been told I am selling. My brother and I are unable to fight anymore. We have no cowhands anymore."

Preacher felt his hackles rise and knew he was about to jump into another fight. It seemed to follow him now.

"I need a job. Am I hired?"

Stammering, Grace Gruber said, "Y …yes."

"I'll not permit it!" Yelled Big John Barker as he slammed his fist on the table. In that moment there was the blurr of a hand and

Barker's fist was still in the air as Teague's gun barrel faced him.

Teague glared at Barker, his face turning red and there was the flash of deep fire in his eyes. "You…don't…have…a…choice!" The last word was all but spit out.

There was the sound of the front door opening and quick footsteps. Several men appeared, only to slow in the face of the gun barrel.

"Barker! We are going to go out that door and to Miss Gruber's ranch. I want no interference." He pointed the gun directly at Barkers' forehead. Barker was reasonable in the face of the gun, but far from beaten. He looked directly at Teague and spoke with clarity.

"We will meet again, Teague."

As the three crossed to the door, men stepped aside. No move was made. If they looked back, however, they would have seen a fierce glimmer of excitement in the eyes of Carson, his hands trembling with restrained excitement.

"Want I should go after him, Boss?"

"No. This throws a bit of a wrinkle in the plans. I need to think."

"What about the men at the ranch house?"

"Let them figure it out. They'll either return alive or not."

Chapter 4

"Mr. Teague, can we really keep our ranch or will we lose it and our lives in the process?"

"Anything really worth having is worth fighting for. To live in submission and surrender is the lot of those who live but have no life."

"You didn't answer my question."

He glanced at Grace, seated with a horse-woman's posture at the reins of the wagon. She was pretty, with the spark of the fighter in her eyes. He brushed the thought aside.

"Mr. Teague?"

"You will keep the ranch. It will take all that I...we...have to keep it, but keep it we will." His look was determined and fierce. She held his gaze, seemingly drawing strength from the man. He seemed to exude confidence and she found herself feeling hopeful for the first time in many weeks. He was a strange man, coming out of nowhere as he had, jumping into the fray and symbolically placing his cards on the table next to hers. She watched him as he rode – on the biggest horse she had ever seen. He rode as a man accustomed to the saddle, yet, there was something else about him. He was a strong man, yet…the spectacles pointed to something else.

After an hour, they came over a rise and Grace pulled up. Before them lay a lush valley, dotted with cattle. In the distance was a ranch house and outbuildings. They urged the horses forward.

Teague looked over the setting, seeing both beauty and strategic components. This valley was obviously a prize, green and with a stream down its middle. There were a couple of visible brooks flowing down the hillside. Water was a natural draw for cattle and kept them from straying as long as the grass was sufficient. It looked to be more than sufficient here, with meanderings of the stream bringing water to more land than if the watercourse were straight. In the distance the mountains changed from mottled brown and greens to blues and grays as they faded above the horizon.

Strategically, both ranch house and out buildings appeared to have a clean field of fire for at lease a quarter mile, and the builder – he assumed Grace and Luke's father - had tended to placement of the buildings as a defensive structure also. As they neared, he could see the strength of the structures, with heavy logs and narrow chinking. There were gun ports built into heavy shutters. Designed no doubt with Indians and outlaws in mind, they were built to last. All brush and trees had been cleared in all directions, except for those in the ranch yard that brought shade and coolness to the buildings. Grace's father was both strategic and practical.

Teague checked his loads as they neared and, replacing his pistol in its holster, reached to his saddle scabbard.

Luke's eyes widened like saucers when he saw Teague pull a seemingly massive Colt revolving shotgun and check the loads. Teague caught the boy's glance and returned a trace of a grin, pointing to his spectacles.

"I don't do well with distance. I prefer close up. In reality, the sight of this gun prevents bloodshed, as most men will not face it unless they are trapped with no way out. Always allow your opponent a way out. After all, in a gunfight you stand a good chance of catching lead also. Never shoot unless you have to, but if you do…make it good, and shoot with purpose and resolve."

Grace's eyes narrowed. "Mr. Teague….you speak like a philosopher and a man to choose peace, but your speed and anger back in town suggests you are a man with a reputation for violence."

His eyes flickered with sadness and, she seemed to perceive, even a moment of despair. Her brow wrinkled with a question.

He paused before answering. With a tenderness unseen till then, he said with a sudden soft coldness, "I have my reasons."

As they neared the buildings, Teague rested the shotgun over the pommel. There were a couple men rising from their seats in the shade.

"Your men or Barker's," Teague asked quietly.

"Barker's."

"Hang back and let me go ahead."

Pulling ahead, he approached the ranch house, the two guards walking in opposite directions to cover him from both sides.

"Hold up, mister!" The speaker was a long faced fellow with large eyes and a drooping eyelid, giving the appearance of almost winking as he spoke. This man, Teague read, was the man in charge here. Without speaking, he shifted the shotgun slightly to cover him and spoke:

"Mr. Barker no longer holds this ranch. Get your stuff and get out."

"Mister, I don't know who you are, but we aim to stay until Barker or McNary tell us to leave."

Both men heard the hammer click and suddenly realized the presence of the shotgun.

Long face spoke. "You can't get us both."

"I don't have to. I just need to get you first."

Even the man's droopy eye widened as he realized this man had no back up in him. A bad man's resoluteness often retreats when faced with true certainty of harm.

The other man spoke from near the barn. "We can take him."

"Hold yourself!" Long face spoke with desperation. "I ain't wantin' to die right here, which is what I'm a fixin' to do if you make a move, Dixon!"

"Both of you drop your gun belts and step back."

"Alright, mister, just don't twitch your finger! I aim to fight another day. I'm gonna drop my belt and I ain't gonna try nothin'. Dixon, be real smart and slow and live to fight another day."

"But Barker will have our hides!"

"Dixon! You'll not have a hide in a few moments!" The belt dropped to the ground.

There was an audible gasp as Teague expertly flipped the shotgun to cover the hesitant Dixon. It was that man's turn to look death in the face.

"Lord have mercy! Don't shoot mister! I'm a'gonna drop my guns!"

"It needs to happen soon." A glance at Teague's face showed intense determination and strength. The man dropped his belt.

"Any more of Barker's outfit here?"

"No, mister, just the two of us. That's the honest truth."

"Grace! You can bring up the wagon!" He hollered.

She pulled the wagon alongside him, but knowingly left a clear field of fire for him should either man bolt. He smiled inside at her awareness.

"Luke, get the men's horses out of the barn. Check their saddlebags and scabbards for weapons. Remove them and bring them to the wagon. Use the side door so you don't get in my field of fire."

The boy hurried to the barn, returning swiftly with the two horses and awkwardly carrying two Winchesters under his arm, and a large and ungainly Navy Colt pistol in his waistband, sagging his pants so that he walked with a wide stance so as to keep his pants from falling.

Teague grinned with satisfaction at the boy as the weapons clanked into the back of the wagon. Luke reached down and gave his pants a firm lift. "Good job, Luke. Now, walk the horses to the middle point between the two men and drop the reins and come back to the wagon." The boy did as he was told.

Turning to the two men, "Now, mount up carefully, and don't give me any cause to think you're pulling some sort of move on me. This finger is getting itchy. Then get out of here."

Both men mounted slow and careful and walked their horses past Teague until about a hundred yards away, when they put the spurs to their mounts and took off.

Chapter 5

Teague eased the hammer and looked around, seeing no signs of any other opposition. After going through the house, and satisfied that they were alone, he took stock of the situation. He had noted the care taken to build this house. It was also a home, with attention to tight joints and with a window in the kitchen and other details that showed a woman's eye and a man concerned about such things. The furniture was simple but nice. The house was cluttered and dirty from the men who had been placed there by Barker.

"Grace, tell me what's going on. Who is this Barker and what is he trying to do?"

"Everything was so peaceful until Barker – or whatever his name is – showed up and started stirring up trouble. At first he seemed to be content to buy out the small ranchers in the area. Then he started showing up in town with deeds from some of those small ranchers, and someone – Brock Mettert - questioned why none of the ranchers he bought them from showed up in town to say goodbye and to attest to the sales. Couple days later a roving cowhand found Brock Mettert drygulched and brought the news to town. Hansen at the dry goods store wondered aloud if the same fate had been the lot of the others. That night Hansen went to his stable to check his stock and didn't return. His wife went out and found him beaten to within an inch of his life and he's been in bed since and doesn't look like he'll ever be the same. Neither he nor his wife will say anything except that it was an accident and he got kicked by a horse. It wasn't a horse, Mr. Teague. Nobody can prove it, but we all know he was beaten at the orders of Barker. Then pa…" She choked up and was quiet for a few moments. "Pa came from rougher stock and he faced one of Barker's men and called him a liar. He thought he was backed by a couple of the hands, but then a dozen of Barker's men spread out to face the three of them and the hands lost their salt and faded, leaving pa to go it alone."

"Did you see it?"

She paused and looked to the ground, nodded, then her face raised and a look of deep resolution sparkled amidst the moisture in her eyes. She gritted her teeth.

"I will see Barker dead!"

"The wages of sin is death..." Teague said softly.

Grace Gruber stared hard at him, her eyebrows knitted.

"Why, Mr. Teague....you are man of many abilities. One moment ready to face a gunfight without fear and the next quoting the Good Book."

He looked at her, and Grace perceived another brief flash of something in his eyes. Was it pain? It was but brief, then the determination returned. The code of the West dictated that she not ask directly, as many a man found anonymity and a new life there. A man was judged by his present and not his past.

"Why do people do this, Mr. Teague?"

"'Those who live according to the flesh have their minds set on what the flesh desires; but those who live in accordance with the Spirit have their minds set on what the Spirit desires.' Barker desires power and money and more than anything else, control of the territory."

"You are a mystery, Mr. Teague. Hard, not afraid to buck powerful people, and you would even be violent if the need arose. Yet, you also are gentle and understanding. You are a learned man. You make me wonder about the life you've lived."

Lem Teague found it easy to talk to this young lady, but as in the past, a sudden wall drew up over his heart when he got close to…close to feelings that reminded him of his past. He shifted the topic.

"So Barker is behind all of this but no one knows why, and if anybody has a hunch they are too scared to say anything. What about your spread?"

She sense the change in him.

"We're the key to the valley. We've got the best of the grass and water, room for many more cows than we run. But I don't understand. The other part of this is that the cattle numbers have been decreasing. In the past, all the area ranchers would have teamed up and searched for rustlers. Now, Barker refuses to let anybody on his land. He has made it perfectly clear that anyone found on his ranch will be shot first and asked questions later. With all the new land he has…come to possess…nobody can get close without risking being on his land and catching a bullet."

"Anyplace on his land where cattle could be held without common knowledge?"

"In the breaks at the far west of his land, at the edge of the mountains. I've heard rumors but never seen it. But nobody can get there. And Barker makes it known that anybody who suggests that he is rustling is calling him a liar and will be called out by one of his men. Mr. Teague, we are not gunfighters here, merely hard working ranchers and cowhands. There are many who can use a gun, but we are not of the same capabilities as the men Barker has around him."

"Is there anybody who has stood up to him?"

Grace hesitated, and Teague noticed.

"Grace?"

"There's an old soldier and Indian fighter way up north. He has the mountain valley below the peaks. Some of the best grazing to be found and no one knows how many mountain valleys his land encompasses or what lays beyond his land."

"How come he's been able to hold out?"

"He has many former soldiers who work for him. Old Man Grizzard only comes to town once a year and many of his cowhands go somewhere beyond the mountains. Rumor is that Barker tried to get through his land once and Grizzard clipped his ears with a Henry and dogged him clear off his land. Barker has made it clear that he intends to own that land."

"This Grizzard…why don't you see him about helping? He sounds like a real fighter."

Again the slight hesitation. He wondered. and wrinkled his brow. She noticed.

"There's some hard feelings…he…he's my grandfather…he and pa had a falling out years ago and we were never allowed to see him. He doesn't know us and might not even know Luke was born. I have a vague memory of him when I was very small….a fleeting image is all."

"Does your grandfather know that your father is dead?"

"Yes. At the funeral I looked up and saw a man far in the distance standing under some trees at the edge of the bluff. When I looked up at the end of the service, he was gone. I believe it was my grandfather."

"You have not seen or heard from him since the committal?"

Grace's eyebrows lifted briefly at the use of the official funeral terminology. Teague was looking at the hills and did not see her quizzical look. She paused, and he looked at her. She shook her head.

"I wondered if the death of father might cool whatever issues remained of the past, but I guess not. Mr. Teague…?"

His eyes met hers.

"Mr. Teague…oh, never mind."

"What is it, Grace?"

"Oh, I just suspect that there is more to you than meets the eye. I hear you referred to as 'Preacher,' and that is curious enough. I know your long handle is Teague, but neither seems to be the word to use on an everyday basis. Mr. Preacher sounds like we are in church, which we are not." She again noted a look in his eyes at the mention of church. "Mr. Teague is too formal for a ranch hand in these parts. Is there perhaps a short handle we might use?" Luke stood looking at him, not unnoticed by Teague.

He paused for a few moments, his eyes roving the hills, taking in the details while his heart rattled inside. He had carefully guarded himself since… Grace sensed something deep and lonely in the man, something which he carried carefully guarded. Her heart reached out.

"I'm sorry, Mr. Teague. We can continue to call you Mr. Teague." She turned away and headed to the well, quickly followed by Luke. Staring at her as she walked away, Teague fought a battle – not a hard one – but a battle nonetheless. Formality kept much at bay that he preferred to keep to himself. Yet, perhaps this was not as big of an issue as he made it.

She was reaching for the bucket when she heard him from behind.

"Lemuel is my given name. You can call me Lem."

She turned, quiet for a moment, sensing the importance of the moment to Teague. She looked in his eyes, seeing a tenderness, yet a strength.

"Very well. Lem it is." She turned back to the bucket as he glanced her way and then returned his gaze to the hills. His mind turned to Barker. Who was this man?

Back in town, Barker sat on the balcony of the hotel. It was a place where he could be alone. He'd made it clear that he was not to be disturbed.

Preacher Teague. Preacher. The man's reputation was one to think about. Reputed to have killed several men, he was known to be also very gentle, with a weakness of helping others in trouble. It could be considered his Achilles heel if it could be used against him.

He had come too far and was not going to be thwarted. He sat and thought with satisfaction how others deferred to him, feared him. It was not always that way. His mind roved backwards in time.

It was when he was a child that John first knew that he must make something of himself. His mother was a whore and his father was just some rambling cowhand or drummer peddling his wares. Just another night of business for his mother. The kids of that town never let him forget it. They called him "whore-boy" and "who-daddy." His mother was too strung out and worn out to care, old before her time. By the time he was ten, he had grown bitter and malicious in his thoughts. He found himself spending time thinking of ways to get back at his antagonists. Yet, he also was small, submissive and weak in reality, lacking the edge to give his thoughts action.

Then his mother died, leaving him with a whole lot less and without a place to call home. He had crawled into the wagon of a passing teamster and they were many miles from home before his presence was discovered. The men made him work to earn his keep and he left at the next decent town. He became as an orphan, and his past was at least hidden. His bitterness remained and he snagged a job with a wildcat rancher who employed those of questionable repute and filled his herds in the dark of night. The men were not kind to him, but he stayed. One man, named Red, laughed at him any chance possible, and John entertained cruel thoughts.

It happened when they were checking the herds one night. Red's horse stepped into a hole and fell, trapping him underneath in a most grotesque manner. His arms were broken so he could not do anything. He cried in pain as the horse thrashed around, begging John to shoot the horse. John managed to get the man's guns and then sat aside and watched from a few feet away as the horse's thrashing tore the man apart. He found himself grinning. He looked at the man and spoke.

"Want me to laugh at you like you do to me?" The man looked at him and begged. John just watched as the man slowly died. Only then did he put the horse down, and only so he could go through the man's pockets. John found that the years had removed all tenderness from him. He later claimed they had separated and that he found the man after wondering why he had not shown up at the rendezvous point. There were a couple of the hands that gave him a look, but nothing was said. The dead man was a loner anyhow and these men were hard.

He later left the ranch and joined a hard case outfit that lived off relatively defenseless travelers and small wagon trains. Then he decided to rob a bank and get some cash to live high and far away. Unfortunately, he had not planned as well as he should, and in the excitement of the robbery a teller pulled a gun and John shot the man. Shot him in the gut and then walked up and shot the man in the head as he lay defenseless. It didn't bother him a bit. As he left the bank, he found himself facing a circle of guns. They locked him up and were waiting for the circuit judge when a young barmaid he had charmed found a way to get the key and John knocked the sheriff out, kissed the barmaid and was gone. A hundred miles away on a stolen horse and penniless, he attempted another robbery only this time failed utterly and was arrested.

The circuit judge just happened to be there and, without any knowledge yet of the previous robbery, a trial was held, he was declared guilty and sent to the penitentiary, where he served a year, then tried to escape and found himself sentenced to five more years.

Released, he found himself gaining experience with mischief and petty crimes. He stayed away from large crimes that drew attention, committing various embezzlements and extortions. He became quite adept and then found himself in possession of a small spread, which he used as a base for growing his herd. He had been fairly successful in rustling, until some high and mighty lawman got too suspicious and decided to skin a cow in town and hang the hide up for all to see the worked over brand. He had left in the dark of night ahead of a posse and caught the rails west. There had been a few other incidents wherein he had been fortunate enough to evade the law. Along the way he had found it necessary to kill an occasional witness. It was especially nasty during that one robbery…He could never go back there again.

This new scheme at West Platte he attacked with special care, taking the name "Barker" after a run in with a dog along the trail west. He'd heard at a saloon about a mountain trail and had tried to work a few cattle through, only to be befuddled by Old Man Grizzard, who had almost done him in. John Barker was determined to succeed, and the rewards were looking good. He had taken over all the area ground for his scheme. All except the Gruber place and the final crown on the whole shebang, Grizzard's place. Get them both out of the way and he had a funnel to and through the mountains and was sure to become rich through a slow gathering across the region. He could take small bunches here and there and fade them into the massive spread he owned, driving them far enough away and right on through the mountains. If anybody questioned his brands on the other side of the mountains, he would pose as a cattle buyer. He would be rich! He had instructed his men to call the town Barkersville. At first the town grumbled, but a few well-placed beatings took care of that.

Chapter 6

Lem Teague settled into making repairs to the ranch buildings. It was quite obvious that there had been no care for the buildings in some time. There was know-how needed for many projects, and he steadily worked his way through what seemed the most important projects. He repaired sagging door hinges, shaky fence posts in the corral, and other items left unattended. In his mind he categorized the items and focused readily on those that might have a play in defense. At the same time, he bristled with waiting. He knew there was a confrontation coming. He felt it in his bones. He was not content to sit and wait for an enemy to show, preferring to take the fight to the enemy. Barker was the enemy.

Chopping wood one morning, Grace came out of the house with a cup of coffee and handed it to him. She looked at him, his shirt off and his muscles rippling. He was indeed, she saw, a strong man, confident and smooth in all motions. She wanted to reach out and touch this man, but knew not to.

Grace Gruber had been raised around the men of the ranch before it all fell apart. She knew that there were times when a man needed to be left alone, times when he needed to be pushed to talk, and times when he reached out. She knew with Lem that there was a deep burden and only the man himself would know when it was time to truly let whatever it was go. Yet she could not ignore the reality that something in this man stirred her.

She also understood the ways of the ranch, having been around her father over the years as he delegated tasks and talked openly to the men, often very coarsely, while she stood nearby. He made a point of not cushioning her, knowing that the West was the West and only the strong survived.

Lem Teague noticed her stability. He had seen in her a steadiness. She showed ability to understand ranch business and needs, indicating that her father must have talked with her and groomed her for her eventual role if and when he was no longer around. She was a strong and capable woman, yet also tender and intuitive.

Since Lem had brought them back to the ranch, they were unable to attend much to the cattle situation, except in the nearby pastures. He and Grace both realized that the distant cattle would have to be dealt with later after action was taken. Right now they all were intent upon sprucing up the place, attending to things that had been low priority for some time, and totally ignored by Barker's men.

He found himself enjoying the routines of the ranch, and especially the time with Luke. Luke was a good worker, seemingly used to the constant tasks necessary to keep a ranch going. Early one morning he went out to the barn to feed and found Luke already there, giving a bait of grain to each horse. Teague leaned against the doorpost and watched for a few moments before Luke was aware of him standing there. Finally, the boy looked over and startled briefly.

"Thought I'd get an early start."

"You're a good man, Luke. The Bible tells us in Proverbs that hard work brings a profit, but mere talk leads to having nothing. You keep working this hard, you'll always have what you need."

"Pa always said that the 'early bird gets the worm.' I don't 'spect I'd like worms that much, but I think he was saying the same thing you just said."

Teague smiled. "You're smart, boy. Real smart."

"Pa also said 'you get as much out of something as you put in.' He was a hard worker." The boy paused and tears welled up in his eyes.

"Your pa was a good man. He taught you well and if you remember the lessons he gave you, then he'll always be with you."

Luke nodded knowingly.

"Your pa knew the truth." He looked into the distance and Luke noticed that Teague's eyes seemed far, far away.

"Mr. Teague? You ok?"

After a moment, Teague blinked a couple times and turned to look at the boy.

"I'm fine…just thinking."

"Mr. Teague? Rex is the biggest horse I ever did see."

"He was a gift to me from an uncle. He's a real gentleman of a horse, and can go all day on hardly anything. If a man has a good horse, it can make the difference in many situations. Now, let's get back to work. Your sister will be calling us for breakfast soon."

Several times he noticed a man in the distance, just sitting his horse. He was sure that Barker had at least one, if not two men watching the ranch buildings at all times. He also knew that Barker would not wait long to possess the ranch he wanted.

He could perhaps get a good shot at the watchers with a rifle, but it was not within the most effective range and really wouldn't accomplish anything. He preferred action, but was concerned with Luke and Grace. He couldn't leave them unprotected nor were they equipped for a siege. He suspected they might lose possession of the ranch if too much of a force came to oppose them. He had already quietly spoken to Grace regarding possible routes of cover should they have to leave. At one point Grace had looked at him, giving him pause.

"You sound as if you would not be here when we leave, Lem, and that it would be me leading Luke out. Are you planning on leaving?"

"If something happens, my best course of action will be to go out there and take the battle to them. In fact, tonight I will go out and scout around. See if I can get a clue to what they plan."

Later that evening, he walked around the buildings in the half light as day faded into night. He noted that the watcher, or watchers, had already faded away and were likely doing what most paid help would do at this time of night – sit around a fire drinking coffee and telling lies.

Grace wandered out to where he stood scanning the horizon. She brushed some wood chips away and sat on the chopping block. He glanced over briefly, and then returned to watching. He scanned the area close by first, gradually moving his eyes farther away. Many tenderfeet would begin with the distance, missing danger close up. Some made the mistake once and the West swallowed their bones and memories.

"What do your senses tell you, Lem?"

"That there are only two watchers and they are settling into their camp right now, preparing some dinner. They expect us to do nothing."

"You're planning something."

"Maybe."

She looked at him, having grown accustomed to his ways. They'd had several conversations since they came back to the ranch.

"Lem, I want to ask you a question. Is it ok to ask?"

"I suppose it depends on the question." He continued to stare into the gathering darkness.

"You haven't always been a gunman, have you?"

"Most men thought of as gunmen had a time in their lives when they were not."

She stared at his back. "You're evading the question."

"Yes." There was something about this young lady that stirred him. Somehow he wanted to tell her, but he was so bottled up. He had survived by sealing things deeply. He knew that she had heard him once cry out in the night when she came to the bunkhouse to see if he needed another blanket. She had been kind enough to pretend she hadn't heard.

""It's ok not to say anything." He could tell she meant it.

They remained silent for many minutes. It was enough to share the time together, listening to the night sounds. Grace was about to stir and return to the house when he spoke. His voice was soft, almost faint, and she could tell that he was speaking from a deep well long sealed. As he spoke, he continued to scan the night. It had turned dark.

"I had a wife and a son."

They both remained quiet, Grace realizing what it had taken for him to give that piece of information.

"What happened?" She asked quietly.

"They're dead."

She somehow knew that this was all he would tell her at the moment.

"I'm sorry, Lem."

After more minutes, she quietly rose and stepped towards him in the dark. Her hand reached out and she was about to gently touch him but stopped. Dropping her hand, she turned and returned to the house.

He had sensed her draw close and it had brought on a combination of tension and yearning, but he remained looking to the night.

His mind wandered in thought as he also kept his senses tuned to the darkness around. Would he ever find happiness again? Could he ever truly love another? He glanced towards the house, hearing the little noises of Grace working in the kitchen, of Luke preparing for bed. He looked deep within.

Some animal moving in the night drew his attention back to the darkness.

His mind spurred to action. He waited a while longer and then sauntered to the barn and saddled Rex. The horse nickered softly and nuzzled as Teague caressed his muzzle and spoke softly to him. Then he dropped the reins and casually walked to the cabin.

Grace was cooking at the stove when he began to check his gun loads, and seated the extra gun in his belt. Then he wiped his spectacles with his shirt.

"Where are you going, Lem?" She sounded anxious.

"I'm going to scout around. I should be back in a few hours. If something happens and I don't return, take Luke and head to the hills like we talked. Don't wait for the shootin' to start."

Noticing her concern and the look in her eyes, he quickly grabbed his hat and stepped out the door.

He mounted and quickly rode off to circle the area where the watchers had last been seen.

With the awareness of a western man, Teague had studied the areas around the ranch and had a rough idea of the ground he needed to cover. He did so and quickly reached a point above and behind where the watchers had been seen. Dismounting, he dropped the reins and took a pair of moccasins out of his saddlebags. They were better for silent approaches, as it was easier to sense sticks and other objects that would make noise. Lem's father had grown up with

61

Chippewa Indian playmates and had learned to move silently through the woods. When Lem was old enough, his father imparted many of the skills to him.

He began to carefully traverse the area. He knew that Rex would stay ground tied and be right where he'd left him no matter what.

Stepping carefully to avoid undue noise, he sensed wood smoke and followed the scent to a dip in the ridge. He crawled carefully up and, removing his hat, peered over the edge.

Two men were by the fire, one rolled up seemingly asleep. The other sat hunched over the remains of the fire, staring into the bright coals. Teague grinned. A man staring into a fire was momentarily blind when surprised from the darkness. It was that moment that could make the difference between life and death. A seasoned and alert man would sit with his back to the fire, staring outwards. Either these were tenderfeet or they had no concerns with surprise. He guessed they were confident they would have no problems. Their boss was the king of the range. So many men, working for a tough man, took on attributes of their boss and developed a false confidence in themselves. It often played out that when the tough man fell, those so attached to him fell themselves or quickly faded off to attach to someone else. Their identity and confidence was never internal but tied to that of another.

Teague heard the sleeping man snore. The other's head was bobbing. He waited patiently till that man, mesmerized by the fire and without fear of danger, finally laid his arms and head on his knees, heaved an audible sigh, and drifted off. He waited a few minutes more, and then slowly made his way down the hill, creeping softly. His father and time in the hills had taught him patience and ways of quiet stalking. A slight breeze caused a subtle stirring that covered any sound. Once, the man laying down snorted and his eyes fluttered. Teague froze and patiently waited for the snoring to begin again. When it did, he came up behind the sitting man and slipped his rifle from beside him in the sand. He rose slowly and came to the other man and took his rifle leaning against a nearby rock. Seeing the man's pistol lying near his hand, he reached and snaked it away and stuck it in his belt. Then, softly making his way back the way he had come, he stopped just before he was out of sight.

He removed a couple of shells from his gun belt and carefully pitched them into the fire. The sitting man startled, but perceiving what he thought were coals popping, went back to sleep.

As Teague quickly worked his way to his horse, he heard the first shell go off, quickly followed by the other. There were sounds of cursing and jumping and scrambling as Teague headed towards the ranch house.

When he neared, he hollered so that Grace would not shoot. She came out of the house with a look of concern.

"Lem! I heard shooting."

"Not shooting, just bullets going off." He grinned, and she sensed a playful sound in his voice. It made her smile. "I tossed a couple shells in their fire after I relieved them of these weapons." Handling the rifles to her, he once again looked to the darkness.

"I'm going back out. I might sashay into town and see if I can find anything out."

"But town is full of Barker's men."

"I'll be careful. You just mind what I said. I'll be back by morning."

She walked to his horse, placing a hand upon the pommel.

"You be careful, Lem Teague." She looked into his eyes, he into hers.

Riding towards town, he wondered for the first time about his travels. At first it seemed he was out for vengeance, then it seemed to be just to get away, but no matter how far he traveled or how high he climbed, his pain was right there beside him. What was he doing? How long must he go on like this?

His past as a preacher had been pleasant, with many invitations and much respect. He was looked to for wisdom and especially the wisdom that comes from above. And yet here he was ignoring the scripture in Romans, "Vengeance is mine, I will repay, sayeth the Lord." He had gifted that wisdom to others through the years, but now here he was ignoring the same words.

Even more confusing to him was why he was suddenly thinking about this. Was it weariness? Or was it the freshness and innocence of Grace? The way she looked in his eyes... He could tell she wanted more from him. He had found himself enjoying the small conversations they had together, the smell of her hair, the way she tried to look nice even when working hard. She was a genuine lady, a lady despite all that had happened, what with her life so shattered. She had a strength to go on.

Perhaps he was jealous? He had not had much strength after Anna and Jimmy died. He had dropped everything and gone on the vengeance trail. Once on that trail, it led to nothing but wandering without any direction or goal. He gave no thought to tomorrow.

Well, now he was thinking. Anna always admired his ability to look ahead and prepare. She would smile that wonderful smile of hers, kiss him and look deep in his eyes with her boundless love. Something within him seemed to be crying out for that peace and stability that once was his...

Was it here? Could he ever feel peace again?

Chapter 7

Coming to the edge of town, Teague surveyed the situation from the trees. It all looked as it had the last time – quiet and tense. He worked his way in from behind some buildings and tied his horse behind the general store. Crouching and looking around carefully, he felt certain he had not been seen. He crept between the buildings until reaching the corner of the saloon seemingly frequented by Barker's men. There were several horses tied to the hitch rail. Looking both ways, he saw no one watching the street. Barker must be confident in his grasp of the town. Or the rest were out rustling cattle.

Stepping to the boardwalk, he peered over the corner of the batwings. A handful of Barker's men played cards at a table to the rear. A couple more lounged nearby, sipping half-heartedly on their drinks as do those who are bored out of their minds.

Hearing a hoof strike stone at the edge of town, he quickly ducked back into the alley. A few minutes later the rider approached and dismounted at the hitch rail. Pausing to look around, the rider stretched and slowly and deliberately came up the steps. He walked as a man with confidence and with wariness. He wore a duster and a slouch hat that hid his face, but there was a wooly beard showing as he came to the light of the windows. Teague saw cavalry stripes on his pants, worn with age and use. The man walked into the saloon and Teague could hear him reach the bar and ask for a drink. There was other muffled conversation and the sound of chairs scuffling quickly.

"You ain't welcome here."

"I jus' wants a drink, den I'se leavin.'"

"You're leavin' right now! You want a drink, there's a creek 'bout a mile on."

Teague walked again to the batwings, in time to see the man turned to the room with his duster pulled back to reveal the butt of a Navy Colt. Three of Barker's men were facing him, hands near their guns.

"Mister, we told you that you ain't welcome in town. We expect you to git!"

He noted the wooly hair but very light skin. The military stripes and the age of the man suggested he was a soldier. He was a mulatto.

But in the eyes of men facing him, he was as dark as his ancestors.

It was obvious the man was facing unfavorable odds, but he was not backing down.

"I come fo a drink – dat's all. Den's I'se gonna leave. I ain't searchin' fo no trouble."

"You ain't gonna drink anything here – now get out! Better yet, maybe we can have a little sport here before you leave."

Another man, having crept below the bar, suddenly reared up behind the man and grabbed his arms from behind. Immediately one of the other men leapt and hit the man over the head with his pistol. The man did not go out, but collapsed to the floor as the man behind loosed his grip. Another kicked the downed man in the ribs. The man groaned. Another had his leg reared back when there was an audible click of a hammer that came to their senses. Startled, they looked to see Teague just inside the batwings, gun at shoulder height and pointed at the man about to kick. Teague's face was red with anger.

"First person that makes any sort of move – any move whatsoever, will get it in the brisket!"

Nobody moved – at first. Then the man behind the bar started to sink down out of sight. With a cross arm draw, Teague drew his Arkansas toothpick and flung it at the man, catching him in the shoulder. The blade sunk deep and the man cried out as he collapsed.

"Bartender, if that man back there makes any move towards a gun, and you don't stop him, I will take it personal." The man, wide-eyed, nodded. It was Kerner, the same man Teague met the first night.

"Now, if you please, stoop down and pull my knife out and wipe it off and place it on the bar." All in the room heard the wounded man cry out as the bartender pulled the knife with effort and wiped it with a bar towel and placed it on the bar, haft out.

Teague pointed to the mulatto. "Now, help this man off the floor to a chair." The men hesitated, until one of the men spoke up. It was the man Teague noted on his first visit who looked like he was inbred.

"It's Preacher! Do what he says, for goodness sakes!" At the sound of the name, the men scrambled to help the man up. The man groaned, rubbed his head and looked up, making eye contact with Teague. Then, reaching to his left side, drew a pig sticker and drove it into the thigh of the man nearest him, who went to the ground screaming.

Teague's face was florid, his eyes wide, but he grinned with a wicked mirth at the victim becoming the attacker.

"Every person here, 'cept for this newly arrived gentleman, needs to be without a weapon, and I need to see belts and guns and knives on the floor at everyone's feet. Immediately!" All quickly dropped their belts, not wanting to face the lightning guns of this man reputed to be as fast as Hardin and Allison. The men were not gunmen, but merely toughs who acted with bravado when around each other, jockeying for position. But when faced with real situations they reverted to their true cowardly selves.

"Everybody except the bartender find a chair and sit!" As one they went to the nearest chairs and sat. The man with the knife wound still sat on the floor gripping his leg.

"Mister, does that floor look like a chair to you?" He spat the words out. The man quickly worked his way to a chair.

"You ok, Jinker?" Teague said to the new-comer.

"I is, Teague. Mighty good to see ya."

"I 'spect so. You able to stand?"

"I reckon." He stood. Teague released his hammer and put the gun in its holster. Reaching to the bar, he picked up his knife, looked at it and, giving the bartender an approving nod, put the knife back in its sheath.

There was a groan and the sound of movement behind the bar, and the bartender seemed to shift as they heard a grunt. Teague looked over and nodded to the bartender.

"Whiskey, please. And one for my friend." The bartender quickly placed glasses and a bottle on the counter. Teague poured, with his head half turned to the other men. Then he handed the drink to Jinker, took his own and with a slight tilt of the glass as in a toast, he downed the drink. One of the men shifted in his chair and instantly found himself facing a gun barrel.

"Mister, did I say move?" The man started to shake.

"Where you headed, Jinker?"

"No where's in 'ticular. "

"Looking for work?"

"Sho 'nuff. Anybody round here hirin' folks like me?"

"I know somebody that will. I work for them."

"I'll grab my hat. What you 'spect we should do wit dese ugly boys?" He drew the word "ugly" out long and the men all looked at him, with barely checked anger. Jinker reached out and grabbed one man off his chair and threw him against the bar, held him with one hand and placed the tip of his pig sticker at the man's throat.

"I said you'se ugly! Now I asks yo 'pinion. Is yo ugly?" He pressed the knife enough to draw blood.

"Yes, I'm ugly!"

"You got's no manners, boy. Say it wit respect."

"Yes, I'm ugly, sir!"

"Dat's better." He let the man sink to the floor.

"Let's get the horses, Jinker." He looked around the room. "I remember faces. If I see any of you out in the street before you hear our horses head out of town, I will take it as a personal affront and will come back for you. Unfortunately, from a distance I will not be able to tell you apart, so I would have to come after all of you. Or I may let Jinker's knife take care of it. Do you get my drift?" Heads quickly nodded.

As they rode out of town, in the shadows stood a man. Carson chewed on a twig, watching the two men. There was a curious sense of excitement as he anticipated a meeting between he and Preacher. It had to happen. He knew he had to test his skills. Yes, there was the chance he would die. He grinned. That was the chance for everyone. But, like others of his ilk, he didn't think of himself as losing, but saw only the pride of winning, of having the reputation of having bested Preacher Teague. He bit harder on the twig.

Chapter 8

They rode quickly at first, Jinker following. A mile or so out of town they slowed.

"I'se glad you was der, Teague. I 'spect it weren't lookin' good fer me."

"What did you think would happen, you walkin' into that saloon?"

"I been on da trail fer two weeks an I was just crazy fer sumpin' to cut the dust. If it weren't fer that no 'count behind the bar I'd been fine."

"As it was, you were almost dead."

"But I ain't, 'cause you done showed up." He smiled. "By da way, I ain't never seen a hoss that big. Where's the Circle-H ranch?"

Teague smiled back. "Circle-H is in Colorado. Cousins on mine. How are you doing, Jinker? It's real good to see you."

"I'se fine. Been a hankerin' to see da West some mo. So's I headed out and dis is where I happens to be. You said yo boss be needin' a hand. Will he hire…someone like me?"

"First off, the boss is a 'she.' And I think she has the character to judge a man by more than what others might."

"What about da other hands? I'se tired of watchin' my back all time."

Teague grinned again. "Well, seeing as we are the only hands, I don't think that will be a problem."

"Jus' two hands? I 'spect this be a small ranch or dey's sumpin' you ain't tellin me."

As they rode, keeping one ear tuned to the sounds of the night, Teague explained all that had happened.

As they neared the ranch, Teague stopped. Making a sign to keep their voices low, he explained the actions of earlier in the night directed at the two men camped not far away. Motioning for Jinker to wait, he crept forward, to find the men still camped in the same spot. Both were hunched over, asleep on their knees. The camp still showed signs of the earlier panic. There was a hole in the coffee pot, which was thrown aside. Teague grinned. In the West, coffee was a necessity and these men would be deprived of perhaps their one joy of the job.

He rubbed his face and pondered other possible shenanigans when he heard a noise a ways off. The men heard it, too, and quickly rose to their feet, the one with the remaining pistol holding it at waist level.

"Go check it out."

"I ain't going nowhere out there alone."

"We'll go together, then." They walked off towards the edge of the draw.

Teague quickly ran to the fire and placed more shells near the coals and covered them lightly with sand. They would heat up slowly and go off in a quarter hour or so, he thought.

He heard the men yelling not too far away.

"The horses! They got the horses! Quick, the camp!" Teague threw himself over the edge of the draw just as they came skidding into camp. Their own tracks were everywhere so they didn't notice the new heel prints.

"Doggone! No horses! Barker's gonna be hot over this and mad as all get out at us!"

The other man flopped before the fire. "Awe, shut up! Might's well sit and get some shut eye. Ain't nothin' we can do. Maybe the horses'll show up."

The other sank down also and both pouted into the fire.

Teague worked his way back towards the horses. He found Jinker standing by the horses, only now there were four. He was grinning.

"My head's hurtin' a mite, but I feel good 'bout dat! We'll let dem go after a fashion."

Teague motioned, "Better mount up. Gonna be more excitement in a few minutes. I left a few presents a mite close to the fire."

As they rode off, they heard the sound of the shells exploding, mingled with cursing and general screaming.

Teague and Jinker grinned at each other in the darkness.

"Twice in a night!" Teague chuckled.

As they neared the ranch buildings, they heard the click of a Winchester hammer cocked.

"Mister, if you intend to live, you better identify yourself!"

"It's me, Grace. Lem."

"Who's the man with you?"

"He's a friend of mine, name of Jinker Jackson. I'll vouch for him."

They heard the hammer being released.

"Come on in, then. Anybody following?"

"I don't think there'll be anybody behind us tonight."

"We heard shooting."

Again the grin. "Tweren't shooting, just a few bullets that got loose near a fire. Sort of got things hopping a mite."

Grace looked at him quizzically, then slowly a grin spread across her face.

"Wish I could see that. Twice in once night. Those boys will be jittery at any sound!" She then walked towards Jinker, extending a hand.

"Jinker, I'm Grace Gruber. You looking for a job?"

"Yes'm."

"You're hired. Now, I expect you both are tired and hungry. Come in the house and eat."

"Ma'am…I'se used to eatin' outside or in da bunkhouse."

"Not here. As long as I'm in charge, you eat with the rest of us…in the house." Jinker looked at Teague, who merely shrugged his shoulders and gestured towards the door.

The next morning, Teague spoke at breakfast.

"I think I need to take a look at the lay of the land around here. I'm gonna do some scouting and see if I can figure something out here. There's got to be something to get Barker so desperate. I'm going to take a ride over towards his land and then off to the mountain valleys."

"I 'spect you'se gonna sugges' I stay here and hep' take care whilst you goes gallavantin' around?" Jinker had leaned back in his chair, thumbs in his braces.

"Yes. Grace, Jinker is a good man and a reliable hand. You can trust him to make wise decisions when the chips are falling." He grinned at Jinker. "Well, he does do some dumb stuff once in a while." Jinker grinned in return.

An hour later he looked and saw a watcher in the distance, now afoot. Who knows where the horses turned up. Maybe went to town. He grinned as he thought of the night the men must have had, and the sleep deprivation they must be experiencing.

Taking an armload of boards from the barn, he made as if he was going behind the barn to fix something. As he saddled Rex he heard steps and turned to see Grace standing in the doorway. She stood looking at him a few moments before speaking. When she did, it was soft, almost a whisper.

"You come back in one piece, Lemuel Teague. I...we need you here." She held herself as she spoke, looking at Rex. Then, she shifted her eyes direct to him. He could see concern in her eyes.

"I'll take care of myself. You remember what I said about getting out of here if things get bad?" His voice had an edge of tenderness.

"I do, Lem. But how will you find us if we leave?"

"I'll find you."

She nodded. He tipped his hat to her and took Rex's reins. As he walked by her, she allowed her hand to loosen and to brush ever so slightly along his arm. He did not fail to feel it, and perhaps slowed his walk slightly.

Keeping the barn between himself and the watcher, he walked his horse a few hundred yards to a wash and mounted, then headed to the distant blue-hued hills and Barker's land. After that, he thought, he might wander up towards Grizzard's – to see what cards the old man might be holding.

He took a circuitous route across the Gruber holdings and over towards those of Barker. He carefully scouted every rise and took advantage of every opportunity to look both before and along his back trail. Once he saw several horsemen riding to the north and, wondering about them, rode a roughly parallel route, keeping as much as he could to ground that would give off less dust. He also shielded his eyes so that his spectacles did not reflect and give his location away.

He saw few cattle, seemingly just a few strays. There should be more – many more – he realized. Just where were they? He had a hunch that the answer was in the trail of the riders, whom he watched closely. He rode on, becoming more wary as a dust plume appeared in the distance. It was another group of riders. A quick look told him that they were headed the same general direction as the group he was following.

Chapter 9

Jinker worked on the barn and made a point of staying close to Grace and Luke, considering the circumstances. He frequently looked around, and was careful to not be caught in any patterns by an observer.

Early in the afternoon, while Luke worked mucking stalls, Grace walked out behind the house where Jinker was repairing wire. She noted the man's coloring and wondered at the connection with Lem. She brought him a cup of water and stood and talked as he drank.

"Jinker? How long have you known Lem?"

"Ma'am, I 'spect nigh on to seven year."

"Where did you meet him?"

Jinker hesitated. "Well, now, ma'am...He he'ped me out onc't."

"Did you know him before he became a gunman?"

He paused. "Yes'm."

"What did he do before?"

"Well, ma'am...he were a preacher." She could tell his hesitancy to reveal any extra information.

"I'm not trying to hurt him, Jinker. I'm just trying to figure things out. What happened to his wife and child?"

Jinker sat down and put the cup in his lap, looked long at Grace and then sighed deeply.

"Ma'am...I don' know how much Teague'd want me to say. But I reckon I kin answer some of yo questions. He were a preacher, one of dem ridin' preachers what had two churches. He'd come by our church sometimes on his way to da other white church, and he got's to be friendly wit us. He even et wit us now an den. You know, out in da churchyard after da church were over. He were a 'spected man, wore nice clothes an everbody knowed him. Well, he he'ped me out, saved my skin one day. I owes dat man."

"His family?"

Looking downward, Jinker hesitated again. "Ma'am...his wife and son was kilt in a robbery of a bank. Not right away, but dey died in his arms inside da bank."

Grace stared at Jinker, her eyes wide, and then the tears began to flow as she pictured Lem holding his wife and son as life left them. The pain. Her hand rose to cover her mouth. Now she understood the deep dark hole he had and the door locked tight. She began to cry harder.

Jinker looked away and watched somewhere in the distance at nothing in particular. He talked softly, almost to himself or no one.

"His church were always full. People loved to hear him preach da Word of God. He was always doin' sumpin' fer somebody, an' it don' make no difference be dey white or any other color. Lem Teague don' see no color – he jus' sees people. He were da kind a man what would give up anyt'ing fer somebody what had a need."

"Dere was dis time when I was bein' 'cused of stealin' a ax from dis white woman's back yard. I didn't do it. I knowed who done it. It were da neighbor man. But when she foun' him wit it, he claimed he jus was bringin' it back cause he found me wit it. It were a out 'n out lie, but he were a white man and so dey come lookin' fer me and takes me to da sheriff and tells him I needs to be locked up an' punished. "

"I were sittin' in the jail cell wonderin' what was I to do. Cain't go callin' both a white man a liar an' a white woman stupid, so's I knowed I were in big trouble. Well, Lem, he knowed me. I done work fer him many's the time. He tolt da sheriff dey was makin' a mistake, dat I were workin' fer him all dat day cleanin' at de church. Well, now, Missus Grace, I know de Good Book say we ain't 'sposed ta lie, but I tinks dey's a time when it's ok in da sight of God. He tolt dat sheriff to let me go so's we could get back to work. Teague knowed dat other man stoled the axe, he tolt me later the man had stolt other things. So's we goes back to da church an' starts to work on stuff so's nobody would t'ink he's lyin' and I been owin' dat man ever since. Lord only knows what dey woulda done to me."

"Did you ever hear him preach?"

Jinker smiled and looked aghast. "Oh, ma'am, dere was no way someone like me coulda gone to his church. But I snuck up to one of da windows of his church onc't on a Sunday jus' to hear him preach. Lord have mercy, da words was like music comin' out an' I like to got in a trance jus' sittin' dere! Lord have mercy – dat man got hisself a gift. But den..." His voice faded off and a pained look came to his face. He looked at Grace and she saw a tear in his eye. He wrung his hands and looked at her.

"His wife and son was in da bank when da robbers came. Dey still don' know what happened, but somebody musta tried to stop da robbery. Dere was dis shootin' and somebody say dey heared his son yell "daddy!" an when it all stopped, Lem was wit' da men runnin' into da bank – him knowin' his wife an' son was in dere. I heared later dat his wife an son weren't dead, but his son died right quick an' his wife died a couple minutes later in his arms while dey was waitin' on da doctor." Jinker paused, looking embarrassed for having told so much to this

83

young woman. But he knew she was different just from having him eat in the house.

"Da next day dey foun' Teague gone, an' dey foun' out dat he bought a good hoss an' guns an such truck at de store. Headed west, dey said. But I knowed…he were goin' after the men what kilt his family. Dey was three of dem. Dey only knowed da name of two of dem…dey was kilt in two different towns, dey say by dis' man with spectacles an' wearin' a gun and faster dan' greased lightnin'. I know it be Teague. I heard dey don' know da name of de other man, but Teague always lookin. I left soon after just to get away an go join dem buffalo soldiers. Now, I come here an' Teague saved my life agin.'" He related a brief account of the saloon.

Grace Gruber stared into the trees, her heart troubled and wanting to reach out to Lem.

Chapter 10

He rode for three hours, alert and eyes roving continuously across the terrain. He especially watched the high ground, knowing that any man worth his salt would have a sentinel at a point where he could see across the miles. The higher he rose, the more his eyes focused upon a rise in the foothills. He cut off the path he was following and took a route that would bring him up behind the rise, with a line of trees between. As he neared, the wisdom of his hunch became clear, as he found a well-worn trail up the back of the slope. He knew that if there were a watcher on the crest, much would depend upon the alertness of the sentinel. If he had been truly alert, he would have spied Teague across the valley. There had been no gunshot, no smoke or any other seeming signal that he had seen from the crest above.

Creeping slowly, he first sensed the horse, which also sensed the presence of a man and snorted. Teague ducked quickly behind an upthrust. One horse – presumable one sentinel. A minute later, the sentinel approached, rubbing his eyes and acting groggy. Finally, giving a cursory look around, he told the horse to quiet and returned whence he came. Teague crept forward, placing a calming hand upon the horse as he approached the bend in the trail. He heard a deep sigh and, removing his hat, peered around the rock. Approximately 15 feet away was the man he had seen, settling again into sleep, and his rifle against the rock nearby.

Teague grinned to himself. Of such situations are the opportunities of life made. A man, tired of watching, sleeping. Well, he would give the man an excuse and also send doubts and wonders into Barkers' camp. He waited until the breaths were deep and the man sound asleep. Creeping on cat feet, he shucked his pistol and laid the handle across the man's skull. He'd be sleeping more deeply and awaken with a good headache. Quickly, Teague searched him and removed all weapons, placing them over the crest to the rear. Then he tied the man and dragged him behind a rock.

Approaching the crest of the hill, he let his eyes only peer over the rim as he surveyed what was before him. He saw that this crest overlooked a deep valley, watered and lush, fading off into the blue of the mountains to the south. In the valley were hundreds of cattle, maybe nearing a thousand as he saw more in the distance. He located a camp and noted the arrival of the two groups of riders. Looked to be about fifteen men all told.

So…this is what happened to all the cattle. And why nobody was allowed on Barker's land. The cattle were held far across his land from any town and any probable visitors. The valley was well-watered and able to hold the cattle, at least for a short time. This number of cattle could go through a lot of grass quickly. Why were they here? There must be the intent of taking them to some market, but not near towns in which the brands might be recognized.

Looking to the distant mountains, he noted a continuous notch as the river entered the hills. There must be some route through, following the river. But why were they still held? Why not move them in small groups as they were stolen?

Grizzard! That must be it! And Grace…her land was a natural funnel to this valley from the valleys beyond.

That was it! Barker was planning a major rustling operation from not only the parts here that he had "obtained," but once he owned all of this territory he could funnel cattle from even farther away into this land - all owned and protected by him. Any seeking to cross his land would be forbidden or, if necessary, disposed of in the vastness of his holdings.

There must be a clear trail through the pass in the mountains. Grace had said how her grandfather was rarely here and that implied there must be another option for Grizzard to sell cattle and buy necessaries. There must be a clear trail through the mountains. That would make Grizzard the holder of the final card in this hand, so the others throughout the area were necessary for the gathering of cattle, but Grizzard was the final ace to make the funnel work to a market where strange cattle and brands would likely be ignored or easily explained away.

A gunshot rent the air. He lurched to peer over the edge at the camp below. A man was standing looking upwards – about ½ mile away, obviously trying to get the sentinel's attention. Teague quickly grabbed the unconscious man's hat, took off his spectacles and walked to the edge to where his shoulders and hat showed, and waved his rifle. The man below motioned him to come down. If he failed to follow orders, the ruse would be discovered soon and he might be swarmed with men. He needed time to get away. Trying for time, he pointed off in the distance back towards the point where the other men had first been seen. He hoped to make them think another group was coming and that his job was not yet over. The man below could be seen gesturing to others and pointing down the trail. Then the man signaled Teague to stay.

Drawing back, Teague went swiftly down the trail, jumping astride Rex and heading down a draw that would keep him out of sight and get him to the hills towards Grizzard's ranch.

He didn't know what was happening back at Grace's place, but he knew that he had come this far and that the few remaining hours would get him closer to a potential answer. Besides, he was confident in Jinker's ability to care for the situation and know the right thing to do.

He had known Jinker for many years, and had been more than glad to be in the right place to help him those years back when he had been wrongly accused. Lemuel Teague had always been torn by all the rules that governed the way Jinker and his people were treated. In fact, his disagreement had resulted in many instances where he had skirted the edge of the law to help, even those who were running from the law. Most were being accused based on color or lineage rather than reality.

He'd developed a great friendship with Jinker after he'd saved him. Then Jinker had gone off to be a Buffalo soldier in the West and they had lost all touch. So many men in those days took off to the West to find gold, to find opportunity, to find a new start. Many found nothing so great, nothing so different than what they'd already had. Some did, however, find a new life where color was a factor, but not as big a factor. The West was different, being a place where you were judged by who you were and not what you looked like. Character was what counted. There were some saloons where Jinker might easily have gotten away with getting a drink, but not here. Teague smiled. Jinker had guts! If it hadn't been for the man behind the bar, Jinker probably would have been ok. He was tough, and had no doubt learned how to survive. Fighting Indians would do that for you. They were some of the best fighters in the world and you either lived or did not. Those who lived, lived for a reason.

Yes, Grace and Luke were in good hands. If a crisis came, Jinker would know what to do.

Chapter 11

"He's known as one of the fastest guns around." Carson was speaking to Barker.

"I'm not afraid of every gunman who comes down the trail, Carson. There's a way to handle men like this."

"What's your plan?" Barker was not accustomed to being second-guessed by one of his hired men and bristled, partly due to the fact that he had absolutely no idea how to handle this particular gunman referred to as Preacher. Until he knew more about him he was unable to plan. He tended to look for the weakness that lay in the heart of every man – and woman. There was an Achilles heel that became a target – sometimes very small – but a target nonetheless. It was usually something that gave the person pause at critical moments, pauses that could mean life or death. He knew that Carson had a weakness. He wanted to be the best gunman and could not help challenging those perceived as better. It was a deep need. So far Carson had successfully beaten all comers, but one day he, too, would meet his match and lay bleeding on the ground. He was itching to prove himself, constantly polishing and oiling his matching .38 Prescott's, so that the brass was like a mirror.

"Well, Carson, the best way to handle this Preacher fella is to find someone who is faster than him. I dare say you'll get your chance at him. We'll see who's fastest."

Carson reddened. "I can beat him!" Though normally very cool in confrontation, Carson found that he was riled at Barker's comments. His hand edged towards his gun.

Barker smiled inside as he noted how quickly Carson was riled. It showed he was eager to prove himself against Preacher. Now, if he could just get them together, maybe the problem would take care of itself. If Carson was not as fast as Preacher, maybe he was a bit more sly. And it didn't matter if Carson lived. He just needed Preacher out of action – permanently. If he timed it right, he might even save wages on Carson. Gunman's wages cut into one's balance rather harshly.

"Relax, Carson." He talked soothingly. "I know you can beat him. I've seen you in action." He watched as Carson relaxed. "What do you know about this Preacher?"

"Not much. He's rumored to have been a real preacher once until something happened to his family. He went after the men who did it, and became a gunman. He's known to take up lost causes and turn them around. He's got a soft spot for kids."

"I see." Barker sat back in his chair, placed his fingertips together and became lost in thought.

As darkness settled upon the foothills, Teague rode carefully, alert to any changes in the shadows. It'd been several hours and he knew the unconscious sentinel had been found – probably long since. Right about now the man was likely being harassed mercilessly for being set upon by some unknown assailant, knocked cold and left tied like a calf ready for branding. Teague held no illusions, however. There would be men on his trail. How fast they came in the dark was a matter of how good they were at tracking. Or, they might have just given it up for the night. But Barker's men knew someone, as yet unidentified, was aware of the valley and the large mass of cattle perched at the base of the mountains. They could not afford to let a witness go. Of course, most of the men were paid hands who would only go so far before drifting off to greener pastures.

Along his back trail he had laid a few rudimentary traps that might slow them down if they were fortunate enough to find and hold his trail. A deadfall here and a rickety rock on a slope might give them pause. Likely, whoever was in charge back in the valley did not have the most capable men under his leadership. Their job was merely to hold cattle and spend their hours in waiting for the next step in Barker's plans. Yet, he could not take it all for granted, as many westerners were excellent trackers. Once, a couple hours ago, he had heard what sounded like a cry along his back trail, very faint and unsure. His instincts told him, though, that someone had tripped one of his traps. He smiled wryly at the thought, knowing that traps not only had the opportunity to slow anyone following, but also confirmed they were on the right trail.

Travel was slow in the darkness. He picked his way carefully along the slopes, grateful that the darkness allowed him to go across open slopes without detection – at least until the moon arose. He gauged the glow over the crest of the mountains in the distance and knew the moon was but minutes from peeking over the rise and illuminating the hillsides. The glow would throw the vision of any pursuers for a few moments as their eyes adjusted, but he needed to get off the open hillside. Seeing a draw outlined by boulders, he hurriedly went behind, finding himself secluded and in the perfect spot to give Rex a breather. He dismounted and loosened the cinch.

Within minutes he was on his way, traversing the draw as it folded into a maze of up thrusts and draws intertwining across the mountainside and through the trees. From a distance it could not be perceived as elaborate as it was in reality. As he approached another bend, he stopped suddenly as he came across a small campfire hidden in a nook of the rock. He crouched, his gun instantly in his hand, his eyes wide and his ears searching for any sound. Whoever had built this fire was expert at concealment. It was not visible until one was right on top of it.

"Ain't no call to be alarmed, mister." The voice came softly from his left as he shifted his gun. It was a deep and smooth voice, without any edge.

"I got some bacon if'n you're hungry. I ain't your enemy. I ain't one of them what's in the valley." He heard footsteps as the voice became a man, stepping slowly into the firelight.

"If'n I was no good, I'd not be stepping out like this." He was a small, wizened man with a plain face except for mostly gray chin whiskers and a handlebar mustache that frizzled into an outcropping of his beard that stuck out quite prominently from his narrow face. He was gangly and walked with a springy stoop. His hat was time-worn and looked to be as full of holes as a worn out union suit. He held his hands out, no weapon in either.

"Light and set, Preacher."

"How do you know my name?" He kept his gun trained on the man.

"I know many things. I know that you are Preacher, and that you are helping Grace and little Luke."

"How do you know?"

"I get around, though not many pay much attention, an' I make it a point of not being seen any more'n I have to. I know you are Preacher, an' it's only fitting that you know my handle. People call me Skerby. Now, if you'd be so kind as to put the gun down or point it somewhere else, I'll get some bacon fryin'."

Teague noted that Skerby had a strange-looking pistol in a shabby holster, twisted half way around his hip. He also noted a similar weapon near the fire. The man noted the looks and smiled.

"LeMat revolver, .42 caliber. This gem 'as got nine shots. Got a middle barrel with a shotgun shell if'n I need it, what ain't likely if'n I kin he'p it. Like to taken my arm outa joint last time I fired it."

"What happened to whatever was in front of you?"

"I were fishin.' Kilt the fish, but weren't 'nuff left to make a bite." He grinned from ear to ear.

"Rifle the same?" He lowered his gun.

"Yup, just in carbine version. Cap an' ball ain't always the best, but I'm used to it."

"What are you doing up here?"

"Well, Preacher, like I said, I get around. An' it just so happens I'se around here." He grinned. "I'se got a habit of sticking my nose out to see what's goin' on. I'se just crazy enough that I gets away with a lot, but I ain't so crazy as most folks think. You sees this here sit'a'tion. You got's this Barker fella wanting to take over the territory, an' then you got's the usual killing of innocent ranchers made to look accidental. They's got's to be a good reason, an' I guess you seen it in the valley back yonder."

"Hundreds of cattle."

"Actually they's near a couple thousand. They's a bunch up closer to the mountains in a box canyon."

"Waiting for a drive, but nowhere to drive."

"'Cept they is a place to go. Through them mountains. They's a way. I ain't seen it all – but I'se seen the start of it. Narrow trail along the branch what comes through the mountains, then down another on t'other side. 'Bout forty slow-goin' miles likely, an' any misstep of man or beast drops you dead in the canyon. Old Man Grizzard been usin' it fer years, takin' his cattle to anywhere he wants on t'other side. Ain't nobody over there asks a question about brands. They figgers just a mixed trail herd."

"Grizzard honest?"

"'Spect so." He grinned again and gave a wink. "Though most ranchers in these here parts

got their start with a little moonlight collectin,'
if'n you knows what I'se meanin."

Lem Teague nodded. Most of the early
ranchers had at times questionable procurement
of animals, where calves from neighboring lands
were brought home. There was a saying that
some cows had an awful lot of calves in one
season. Or after the war, when cattle left to breed
without branding in wilder areas were seen as
fair game for whomever had the wherewithal to
ferret them out and take them to market. Many a
rancher found these wild cattle and moved them
to their own lands. Of course, now these cattle
were rare and any moonlight collecting involved
changing of brands with a running iron or a quick
move from rustling to market. This was often
evidenced by tired cowhands with more money
than usual. A few cows disappearing now and
then were nothing unusual nor much worried
about. At first, a few head were given to passing
Indians, then an occasional head was hurriedly
butchered – usually at night – by a passing
wagon train of settlers. Then the ranchers
themselves even parted with a cow now and then
for a family with children needing milk. Even
tough as nails ranchers, after fighting Indians and
various breeds of bad men, still had a heart.

"There may be some men behind me, though
I think they'll likely wait for morning."

"I been 'round, and I don't think any o them thar hired hands is much to prowl around at night. Here, finish off the coffee."

"What's your play in this, Skerby."

"Oh, I dunno....I'm jus sort of moseyin' aroun' seeing how the cards is dealt. Mind you, I got's a soft spot for Grace an' her lil' brother. Ain't in me ta see such as them come to hurt."

Teague's eyes bored into Skerby, evaluating the man. He had been known in the past for his ability to see the true nature of men, and his mind and heart told him that this man before him was true to what he said. There was something else, however, that the man was not revealing. But it was the way of the west – what a man is now is more important than what he was. Skerby, like many, had a story behind him, a story one never asked, a story only heard when volunteered. He lapsed into himself as he stared into the darkness. His thoughts ventured, hesitantly, into the past. Hesitantly, because it took an act of will to look backwards and push aside the vivid pain. He realized he was a very different man now from what he had been. Once prominent in a community, here he was, wandering, looking for – for what? He didn't know. He remembered once seeing a horse with colic, frantically walking the yard, trying to get away from the pain. Yet, no matter how fast it walked, the pain was always there.

He felt the same. The wandering of the past few years had not eliminated the pain. What was he doing, thinking that the constant movement would help? It never did. He still dreamed, still woke up. There was a deep emptiness inside. And there was still that one other man involved in the robbery. A man without a name.

And then there was the anger. It was so close to the surface that he was unable to hold it back. Any little offense set him off, and especially when he found someone being taken advantage of - someone who was innocent and unable to help themselves. Like Grace and Luke.

Luke! Quite a little man. Pain flooded Teague's thoughts. His own son would be near eight by now, just a couple years older than Luke.

Teague shook his head. He suddenly became aware of Skerby looking at him.

"You ok, Preacher?"

"I'm ok." He was embarrassed by his loss of control. "We best get some rest."

"We kin sleep easy, Preacher. My horse is bout as wild as a long-haired banshee. Ain't nothing comin' close 'thouta warnin.'"

Chapter 12

Dawn found Teague and Skerby tightening their cinches and preparing to move out. Ever since they arose, Teague saw the man casting glances at him. As they were mounting, Skerby finally spoke.

"Awful hard to get a good night's sleep with a man like you aroun,' carryin' on half the night." He had been disturbed more than once by his new companion crying out in the night, tossing and turning.

"Night is not my best time." He was short with Skerby, pushing the conversation elsewhere. "Know anything about the best way to Grizzard's ranch?"

"That's where I'se headed! I ain't lookin' fo'ward to meetin' the cantankerous feller, though. I hear tell he don' like bein' 'sturbed. Gots some sorta big burr under his saddle. Poison mean, I hear, and likely to shoot first an' ask questions later. But I kin tell you got's yer mind set an' I guess if'n it'll he'p Grace and Luke, I kin he'p you. Now, mind you, I don' like to go in a direction no more than I gotta. I prefer to wander sideways an' this and that. But I'se gonna go 'gainst my nature here. Prob'ly get us both kilt."

Heading further into the crags of the mountain, Skerby obviously knew where he was going. Several times they paused, dismounted and looked to their back trail for extended periods. They saw no signs of being followed.

As they drew close to the mountains, Skerby became extra watchful, seemingly nervous. He paused more often, cocking his head this way and that, listening.

"What do you know that I don't know, Skerby?"

"'Ol Grizzard's got men outn' here what's likely seen us already. I jus' hope they's not too quick on the trigger."

"You've been here many times?"

There was a pause. "'Nuff to know I don't wanta be here." His answer was evasive. Teague pondered the man. Where did he come from? Why did he know the way to Grizzard's mountain ranch? Why was he so hesitant?

"Are we on Grizzard's range?"

"Likely. Hard to tell where one man's range ends an' another's begins out here. People always arguin' over such things. Never a good answer." As he was speaking, his eyes were roaming wide, moving swiftly from side to side.

They rode a good part of the day. It was slow going, as the trail Skerby was following went hither and yon. They stopped for a midday rest and gave the horses a good breather. Even Rex was winded, as they climbed in altitude and constantly switched back and forth. Eating jerky during one stop, Skerby paused and stared off into the distance. They were behind a large boulder, so he could not see what the man was looking at.

"What do you see?"

"Thought I seen something move away off ahead. I think we can figure we's been seen, an' I hope it's the right people. Then agin,' I ain't sure any of this is all good."

Mounting again, they rode for another hour, and both men kept a constant look to the country around. They passed through some trees and came to a narrowing of the trail, such that they had to slow and go carefully through a notch in the boulders.

Just as they came through, they heard the click of multiple cocking hammers.

Back at the ranch, Jinker and Luke had ventured out a ways and worked to clean a spring that Barker's men had caved in as part of their efforts to get Grace out quickly. As they cleaned,

Jinker stopped frequently to scan their surroundings, his well used and scarred .44 Henry close at hand. Luke was becoming a fine hand in his own right, imitating Jinker as he rose now and again to glance around. Once, they both popped up at the same time, looked in each others' eyes and laughed.

"Jinker, you look different."

"I'se been told dat."

"You look like…well…but then you don't." Feeling awkward, Luke turned red.

"Well, I realizes dat. I kinda looks halfway, don' I?"

"Yes."

"Well, dat's 'cause my grammy were a slave, and her white massa done made her his…uh…wife. Den dat kid what she had were my pappy, and he were real light, den he, uh…married, an'…well…anyways, dey is a way it turns out an' I looks mostly white but not all da way."

Luke had listened with brows furrowed. "I see. Is it kinda like my little white spotted puppy? Pa once told me that it's momma was a brown curr dog that stopped by and its momma was mostly white?"

Jinker stared at the boy, his features slowly turning from stern to a wide smile. "Well, I ain't got no spots, but I 'spect you 'bout got's it, 'pecially dat part bout da curr dog. But I t'inks we needs ta finish dis up here. 'Bout time fer some edibles, an I t'inks yo sister is 'spectin' us fo long."

As they rose to leave, Jinker held his hand out to Luke to help him up. Luke smiled and grasped the man's hand. With a quick flick, Jinker flipped him to his back, where Luke laughed as the man hopped like a horse and whinnied.

A shot rang out and sand flew at the mulatto's feet. Instantly he threw Luke aside and grabbed for his rifle. He glanced around, eyes wide with a combination of anger and the fear of the hunted. Fifty yards away one of the men watching the ranch sat his horse, grinning.

"Well, boy." He drew out the words. "I hear tell you're a tough one. You din't look so tough then, just sorta funny grabbing an' lookin' around. I coulda nailed you."

"You coulda hit dis boy! Wha's you trying ta do."

"Don' sass me, boy. I don' take to such as you actin' uppity."

Jinker glanced at Luke and whispered. "Stay down, Luke."

"I think I'd like to trim your ears a mite, boy. Teach you a bit of a lesson." He clicked the hammer back on his rifle.

Jinker had been in many rough situations in the past, and knew that this would get nothing but worse. The man's Winchester lay across the saddle pointed right at Jinker. If he shifted a pace

105

to the right, the man would need to shift to bring the gun back in line. The army had drilled him and he had drilled himself for moments such as these. He threw himself wide to the right, taking him further away from Luke, and came up with his elbow in the dirt sighting the Henry for only an instant as he felt the impact of the bullet in the dirt next to him. His own shot clipped the man's saddle horn and ripped upwards into the man's belly and windpipe. Hitting the ground, the man squawked and clutched at his throat and stomach. In just a few moments he spasmed and lay still.

Luke sat, wide-eyed, staring at the man, then at Jinker.

"You ok, Luke?"

"He was trying to hurt us – to kill us – wasn't he?" Tears were in his eyes.

"He were aimin' to hurt me. Prob'ly woulda left you alone."

"They killed my pa, Jinker. He mighta been one of the men that killed my pa. If he hurt my pa, he'd hurt me."

"Mebbe. I reckon you be knowin' a lot, Luke. I never 'splained nothin' like this to a kid, not sho' how.

"I ain't gonna look at the man any more, Jinker. My pa once had to kill a coyote that was attacking a calf. I think that man was sorta like that coyote." He wiped his eyes and turned away.

Jinker looked at Luke with pride. The boy is really quite a man, he realized. Out here in the

West a boy grew up fast at times – had to – to deal with the conditions of this yet raw country. Jinker looked around quickly.

"Git our t'ings together, Luke. I'se gonna send dis boy home wit' his horse." He went to the man's saddle and removed the slicker and, placing it on the ground, rolled the man into it. He quickly picked him up, threw him over the horse, and tied him on. The he gave the horse a swat and the horse ran off. The horse had become accustomed to wherever his lodgings had been and would take the man to wherever that was. The man's rifle lay on the ground, so Jinker grabbed it and quickly went to Luke. Mounting their horses, they spurred for the ranch.

Chapter 13

Almost in the same instant as the hammers clicked, a gruff and serious voice calmly spoke from off the trail.

"Hands up!"

Teague and Skerby pulled up, making a point to keep their hands in front as they held the reins high.

"I said hands up!" The voice was even more commanding.

Both men let loose of their reins and put their hands above their heads. Four men slowly entered the trail, two from behind, one in front and one over the crest of a boulder to the high side of the trail. He looked down on them, his rifle pointed at both but neither of them. He rolled his chew and spat on the rock at his feet. Spatters landed on Teague's face, causing him to wince, a reaction not unnoticed by the man wiping his chin with his sleeve.

"You're on Grizzard range. We've been watching you. We seen enough to know you ain't with Barker's outfit. If'n you was, you'd be dead already. Name your outfit and your reason for being here!"

"We came to see Grizzard." Teague spoke clearly and without fear. A consequence of his life situation, he knew that if gunplay started, he may die but he would take someone with him. It gave a confidence that shown in his face and tone of voice. The man on the rock noted this and had the wisdom to perceive it for what it truly was. He raised his eyebrows.

"Well, mister, that's half the answer."

"We ride for Grace Gruber."

"What's Gruber hands doing out here?" He looked at Skerby, who looked from the man to Teague. The man's rifle tilted to Skerby, indicating the need for an answer. "You working for them now?"

"I don't work for nobody."

Teague spoke. "Miss Gruber's been losing cattle and Barker's been trying to force her off her ranch. We're trying to help out."

"Old Man Grizzard ain't got nothin' to do with it. You can turn around and leave now."

"Mister, I don't know who you are, or what your role is with Grizzard, except that you must be his foreman or something. But you and I

109

know that Grizzard has more at stake in this than you're letting on."

"Grizzard can take care of himself and that's all he plans to do."

"We'd like to talk with him."

"Mister, you're being rather bold for some saddle tramp with four guns on him."

"Grizzard has a lot to lose."

"What's that supposed to mean?"

"It means we need to talk to Grizzard."

A Pause. Teague smiled inside. He had a hunch that at least this one man knew more than he was letting on.

"I got my orders that no man comes across the range."

"Orders have to be interpreted based upon the situation. We've got information for Grizzard."

The foreman looked to be fighting a battle inside. Teague could tell he had won.

"Take their guns, tie their hands in front."

One of the hands spoke up. "Daggone! Look at the size of that hoss!"

When Jinker and Luke rode into the ranch yard, Grace could tell something was amiss. She came out of the front door with her 20-gauge shotgun loaded and ready. They came to a halt near her.

"You two are riding like you been chased by a ghost!"

"Might's well be, Miss Grace. We done had some trouble, an' I kilt a man dat was shootin' at us."

"One of the men watching us?"

"Yes'm."

"Did he shoot first?"

"Yes'm, but it's worse dan dat. I loaded him on his hoss an set him free. Onc't dey figure it out, dey's gonna be on da way. An' it don' make no difference if he shot first."

"What is it, Jinker? He tried to kill Luke."

"Well, he's white an' I is what I is."

Realization hit Grace. Within a few hours of the man being found, there would be a posse, all Barker's men, of course, coming and claiming the man was murdered. They would stop at nothing, and without a solid law in the area, they would make short work of Jinker, especially with him being mulatto, and he would hang from the nearest tree.

"Any sign of Lem?"

"No ma'm." That meant if she sent Jinker away, there was no man to help defend the ranch. Her heart sunk. They would have to leave. And quick.

"Jinker, saddle my horse. Take things we might need for a few days out. Luke, let's grab some things."

111

They rode out ten minutes later, seeing no observer. The second man was probably on his way to town with the body. She could imagine the ruckus that would result among Barker's men. Barker was astute enough to know that this might be the opportunity he needed, with a white man being "murdered" by a mulatto.

Indeed, Barker was quick to see the possibilities.

When Porter rode in with Robards over the saddle wrapped in a slicker, Barker had ordered Carson to bring them quickly to the livery. There they unwrapped Robards and discussed what to do next.

Letting his men get incensed, he realized that this might be the answer to possession of the rest of the range he needed. If the anger was fed, there might be people troublesome to him who were "unfortunate" enough to die in the process. And if a woman were one of them….he just needed to be sure he was nowhere in the vicinity. Only a few of his men knew how far he'd go to take over the ranches. He sent the word that he was to speak to his men from the steps in front of the saloon. He intended the townsfolk to see the theatrics also.

As the men gathered in the street, he stomped to the steps, halting and making himself look what he believed was both angered and hurt.

Townsfolk gathered nearby, but none came too close.

"Men, one of our own has been brutally murdered without provocation. I hoped it would not come to this, but I've also just been informed that this killer is a mulatto named Jinker Jackson. Some of you know what he looks like since he's caused problems already. Not only is he uppity, but also he's a cold-blooded killer. You are going to go out in two groups and I want this man found. Anybody with him is to be considered an accomplice, and if any" - he stressed the word - "any opposition whatsoever is given, there is to be no mercy shown. We will not allow this man to run free. Next thing is he will be after our women and children." He said this for the benefit of any townspeople within earshot. Then he took out his kerchief and wiped his eyes. He spoke with deep conviction and passion. "There is a good chance that he has already murdered Grace and Luke Gruber. He is to be brought in dead or alive."

Calling for his horse, he made a point of looking distraught. He mounted and the men rode out.

Chapter 14

When the group came to Grizzard's ranch, it was sudden. Turning a corner in the trail, they came to an outcropping in the shoulder of the mountain. Looking down, there was a sight that few had seen in recent years. Grizzard's land was indeed a prize. The valley stretched for miles along the small river flowing out of the mountains beyond. It was lush, if narrow. There was the natural barrier of the slopes to keep the cattle in the lower valley, for cattle will naturally keep to the easiest forage. To the south, Teague could see the valley narrow, so the end towards Barker's holdings would be easy to monitor.

Their escort appeared to be men capable of meeting any situation. They were solid men, and well armed. As they descended towards the ranch buildings, Teague noted the fortified nature and layout of the place. The buildings were placed such that taking one building was unlikely without exposure to gunfire from another building. It was obvious that this was not an easy target for any takeover. They could see men in the valley and all had dissipated, likely to prearranged positions.

As they came within a half mile of the buildings, a group detached themselves from the main buildings and rode to meet them. As the two groups converged, Teague noted Skerby looking nervous and casting glances at the men around him, as if seeking to escape. Teague's brow furrowed and the man nearest Skerby noted the looks and drew his horse nearer, cutting off escape.

A man riding a beautiful stallion rode in front of the approaching horsemen, who spread as they neared into a modified phalanx, with practiced precision. The leader was an immense man, mostly gray but very erect and with a commanding presence. His eyes were circled by the wrinkles of one who spent much time looking and squinting. His nose was classic roman. Teague noted his full beard, but also saw the man was dressed as any other man on any ranch. It was his presence that stood out. He was the obvious leader and clearly all understood and deferred to him.

Old Man Grizzard was indeed no longer young, but he was far from weak. He glanced angrily at Skerby, then pulled up.

"What are these men doing here, Mr. Lewis?"

"Sir, we found them on the mountain trail. This one"- he nodded toward Teague – "indicated he had information for you." Grizzard eyed Teague coldly for a few moments.

"Untie their hands. Return their guns. Mr. Teague – you may ride with me." Glancing at Skerby, he paused. "I don't know why you showed up, but I'll deal with you later." He quickly rode off, expecting that Teague would follow him and his men. Teague did so, glancing quizzically at Skerby. The other men waited to escort Skerby in another direction, towards the buildings.

Teague noted the military bearing of the men, as well as their strength and confidence.

"I hope your information is really as crucial as you indicated to my men, Teague." Riding to a promontory overlooking the house and corrals, Old Man Grizzard slowed and with a gesture waved the men away. They moved out of earshot, some of the men continuing down the valley, leaving three who watched closely and had weapons ready to hand. They were placed in such a way that they could shoot Teague without hitting one of their own. Teague did not miss the detail. These men were more than average cowhands.

"Sir, I think I can presume you know of this man Barker who seeks control throughout the valley?"

"I know of him. What's your role in this?"

"I work for Grace Gruber." Grizzard's eyes flickered briefly.

"And?"

"Barker has tried to force her off the ranch. She's struggling to keep them at bay. Her pa was murdered by Barker's men. Thought you might like to know."

Grizzard looked for a full minute at Teague's face, holding eye contact. He was a man of much self-control. Finally he looked off across the valley.

"What happens in the valley is no concern of mine."

"Once they have the valley, they'll be headed here for the pass. Barker intends to have it."

Grizzard looked stern and there was fire in his eyes. "What he wants and what he gets will be two different things altogether. This valley and the pass through the mountains are beyond his reach. In case you haven't noticed, my men are mostly men bloodied in the war, men with grit and determination. They are men who prefer the solitude this place guarantees, a place where none ask questions of their past. They are hard men, Teague. Several have wives here, choosing their wives carefully to find those also who like solitude or who have something of their own that they wish to be forgotten. My men meet any needs by going north through the mountains, and that includes all sales of cattle. I have absolutely no need for the valley people to the south nor any person therein."

"Luke is a good little boy."

"Why should I care about this Luke?"

"He is your grandson." Grizzard's eyes widened.

"I know of a granddaughter, but not of any grandson."

"He's six years old and in need of a man's guidance. He's quite the lad, with the makings of quite a man someday, if he gets the right guidance. With your son dead, that responsibility belongs with you, as his grandfather."

Grizzard paused and stared across the valley. After a few minutes, he spoke.

"I gave up my son and his get years ago."

"I don't know what it was that came between you and your son, but there are two of your grandchildren down there who are in danger and needing help. Grandchildren."

Another pause. Then Grizzard spoke, staring off into the distance.

"Malachi chose to marry that girl from town. She despised me, hated me for what I had here, and kept egging my son on to get his share. He began to work behind my back, maneuvering as she ordered, even to the point of trying to get me killed. She died of the fever, but my son I could

118

never trust. He was weak. When all this happened it broke my wife's heart. I watched as she pined away and then I just found her dead one morning. She just couldn't understand how any son of hers could be so weak and betray his own parents."

"Well, Grace is not weak. Her father imparted some great qualities in her. He may not have been a good son, and he may have been weak in ways, but he must have have rebounded after his wife died. Grace has backbone, she's beautiful, and I think she has staying power that her father didn't have. I think she'd make you proud. She can run the ranch." There was silence for a few moments. "It was Teresa of Avila who said 'Christ has no body here on earth, no hands but yours, no feet but yours.' I would suggest that right now, He has no horses or men but yours to help your granddaughter."

Grizzard looked long at him, eyes squinted.

"Like many men in the West, you are somewhat more than what might appear."

Another pause on Teague's part. "You're right, sir."

The man glanced at him. "How long have you been in the valley, Mr. Teague?"

"About a month."

"How do you know so much about her in such a short time?"

This time is was Teague's turn to pause. His mind raced into the past and his ways of life.

119

"I...I have a gift of reading people's hearts and their true character."

"Tell me something that will prove to me you have the skill to tell character.

Teague's eyes widened, then narrowed. He sat quietly as they both stared across the valley.

"They call me Preacher."

He expected a response from Grizzard, but received none. They sat quietly for a few minutes, with Grizzard's eyes squinted off across the valley, as if working on some issue in his mind. Teague said nothing, letting the man's mind work. After what seemed like an eternity, the man quietly spoke.

"Grace is beautiful you say? And Luke, what kind of child is he?" He had spoken without looking at Teague. What Teague had revealed apparently meant something to Grizzard.

"Grace is a beautiful woman and a woman with which any man would be proud to ride the river. Luke is an intelligent child, quick to grasp, willing to be a man, but innocent and needing guidance. Both would make you proud."

Grizzard nodded. "I know of you, Teague. I know who you are and what you are. I know your past. Not many men do. I know it because there is more to me than you perceive. I know of your reputation for unnatural ability to see people for who they are. When you see me, what do you perceive?"

"I see a man who has accomplished much. A man who appears hard and commanding, a man who has built something to last, a man incredibly capable, but who deep inside has a soft spot and a desire to do what is right, despite past grudges."

The man chuckled without a trace of a smile. "You are, indeed, a man of uncommon skill. Tell, me, what did you note about my reaction to your friend Skerby?"

"There is something between you, something hard, something in the past."

"He is my brother. Hard to believe, with the difference in our builds. There was always difficulty between us as we grew up, and it never got any better. We barely tolerate each other, and it's been three, four years since we've seen each other."

"He can't be all bad. I found he has been keeping tabs on Grace and Luke and then he brought me here."

Grizzard grunted.

"We'll never be friends. It's too late."

Teague said nothing. Again, both stared off across the valley. Finally the big man spoke.

"Too late to ride out tonight. Let's head down to the ranch."

Chapter 15

The Ranch buildings were strong and built to withstand both weather and misguided men. The walls were thick and windows were narrow with shutters thick enough to stop most bullets. It was a place that could be held with just a few men, if needed. Gun ports were placed to eliminate blind corners and any attackers would have no protection.

Teague admired the handiwork. He learned much about Old Man Grizzard and his outfit in just the few minutes he walked his horse to the barn. The man was fastidious with his workmanship, with joints tight and even the water troughs were built with heavy planking. There were men at key spots throughout the buildings, men obviously there by Grizzard's prearrangement.

As he looked across the valley, he saw that even haystacks were small and distant from one another. The whole setup showed strategy and resourcefulness.

Grizzard pulled up at the barn. Skerby was already there, with two men watching nearby.

"Ronson! See that these two men get what they need. And tell the men they can relax. This man is no threat. Teague, I expect you'll join me for a drink after dinner." Teague noted that Skerby was not invited.

Settling into the bunkhouse, Teague and Skerby found bunks in the back, and shook dust off old blankets before unrolling their bedrolls. The men soon heard a brief beating of a spoon on the bottom of a pan, and Grizzard's men arose. Along with the others, Teague and Skerby filed out and gathered around the table of the cook shack. Beef and beans and fresh bread slathered with butter was a meal fit for a king and Teague could understand the rumored loyalty of Grizzard's men. It was true that an army marched by its stomach, and these men lived in plenty. His eyes opened wide when he saw the cook bring out massive berry pies to which the men applied themselves without any comment. It was likely that such fare was nothing unusual for these men. Definitely content men if this was any indicator. There was very little small talk as the men helped themselves liberally. When satisfied, the men sat back a minute or two, belched and slugged down a cup of coffee while picking at their teeth before nodding to the cook and leaving.

After dinner he joined Grizzard beside the fire in the main house and shared a glass of home brew. While they spoke, the man named Lewis came in to update his boss.

"Boss, we'll be ready at first light."

"Who do we have coming?"

"Darter, Hoke, Blackie, Peachy and Moose."

"Good. I'll have Cookie pack us some grub."

"Already done that."

"Good job, Mr. Lewis." The foreman left the room.

"Is that all the men you can spare?"

Grizzard chuckled. "With this group of men I would ride into the mouth of hell. I have, in fact, done so more than once. Each of them is worth three men. One of the points of strategy, Mr. Teague, is that too many men can be a problem. It creates a situation wherein men lose that crucial instant's advantage by a pause to identify their opponent. That pause can make a difference – a life or death difference. I have kept my men alive over the years by being careful and never running pell-mell into the fire."

"Yes, sir."

"Mr. Teague – or Preacher. Whatever you want to be called. You have succeeded in your purpose for coming here. I guess there is that within me which must indeed reach out to my grandchildren. It is all in the hopes that the apple does, indeed, fall a long way from the tree. Perhaps I have softened with age."

"You won't regret it, sir. Grace is a marvel and very beautiful. But it doesn't go to her head. She is wise beyond her years."

Grizzard noted the look in Preacher's eye as he spoke of Grace. He grinned inside.

"Are they alone at the ranch?"

"No, a good man is with them. His name is Jinker and I have known him for years. He is solid and will look after them. He is the only reason I felt I could venture here."

"I sure hope all is well. It'll take the best part of a day of hard riding to get to that ranch."

"I pray all is well."

"Morning's going to come early, better get some shut-eye."

As Barker's men had ridden out of town, they naturally took with them those timid souls of the town who were unable to stand by themselves and who needed belonging to keep them going. Unfortunately, they also found themselves tied to a beast from which it would be hard to escape. They followed Barker because he was there to follow and they were doomed by their character and need to follow. Trapped in a sense. Also riding with them were those who had an innate desire to lord it over others, and who found Barker as the catalyst for their cruelty and who gave them the license to act tough and superior. They were so caught up in their own desires that they missed a most important fact: Barker's desires were greater than their own and he would sacrifice any of them and any number of them to get what he wanted. He treated them as if they were part of something, when in essence they were merely disposable pawns in his life's game of chess. There could be only one winner, and it would be him.

There were also those in town who feared him and all he stood for and would not risk his ire or that of any of his men. They were those who would not commit to him, but who would not oppose him in any way, shape or form. They merely lived in that dim and narrow path that was life but was not truly living. They offended no one, made no marks, left nothing but a few trinkets behind to indicate they were ever more than a name on a tombstone.

And then there was yet another group. They were those who despised all that Barker stood for and all that he had brought to this once peaceful and united town. They recognized that they were outgunned and could not stand by themselves, so they quietly bided their time. They recognized each other amidst the crowd and knew the danger of standing together, of seeking each other out, but glances conveyed much and a quiet fellowship developed. And a biding of the time until…

Kerner had been the barkeep for five years. He had found West Platte after several years of feeling lost and moving from town to town in a desultory manner looking for something he knew not what. Then he wandered into this quiet hamlet and found what he was looking for. He was happily if hesitantly welcomed and took the job as barkeep. He loved his job for the information he gained from it, listening to all who stood and received the drinks he provided. Barkeeps were seen as invisible at times, everybody's friend at others. Men talked about everything going on, good and bad, and as long as he kept their drinks plied and wiped glasses and looked other directions, it was if he didn't exist. Interestingly, when a man bellied up to the bar in a melancholy mood, they often would summon him and bleed their guts to him if no one was around.

He knew the groups. He knew the bad ones. He knew the weaknesses and secrets of many men. And he knew better than to let them know he knew, for that would be his end – likely in some dark and dirty alley or, worse yet, just his sudden disappearance. Yes, his job was that of delicate balance.

And yet, beneath it all, he was a proud man. He had served in the war as a private under J.E.B. Stuart. He may have lost some of his hair and wasn't a big man, but he was indeed a man. He had been schooled in right and wrong and while he had stood by quietly up till now as Barker became the ruler of the roost, figuring he would eventually move on, he had come to a point where his inaction was squelching his heart. He knew that Barker was claiming to be after the mulatto, but that there was firm intent that the opposition of Grace and Luke Gruber would also be ended. He heard Barker talking with one of his men at one point, as he polished glasses in anonymity, about finding a way to eliminate the two without incurring the wrath of local society and chivalry. It was still the code of the West that women were sacred. Any man molesting or deliberately harming a woman, girl or child was subject to a quick hemp necktie party. Barker was indicating his approval of murder...the murder of Grace and Luke.

He also knew that this man known as Preacher had started something, something that brought hope to the town and the situation around the territory. People were brightening, smiling a bit more, and the death of Barker's man at the hands of the mulatto Jinker brought secret smirks and a grudging appreciation and acceptance of Jinker Jackson. Even last night when he was alone, he helped himself to a shot of the better stuff under the bar and raised his hand in salute to the man.

He wondered, where did this Barker come from? He must have a history somewhere. Though Barker would not likely be his true name, it must have cropped up somewhere in the recent past. And Kerner knew people through his war service and through his travels.

As Kerner stood on the walk before the saloon, having listened to Barker and seen the men ride off, his mind resolved itself to what must be. Walking into the saloon, untied his apron and tossed it on the bar as he proceeded to the storeroom at the back. Here he had a small curtained-off room as part of his compensation. From under his cot, he grabbed a dusty holster with a Navy Colt and checked the loads. Belting it on, he went out the back door and began going behind the buildings to certain doors and knocking. At each door a few words were said. His last stop was the telegraph office, where he noted that the telegrapher was not present, and remembered seeing the man ride off with Barker. Drawing from rusty skills from the war, he sat to the keys, tapped out a message and waited for the confirming reply. He then left the station.

A chain of events had begun.

An hour later, at a small meadow outside of town, two dozen men and women gathered. Kerner welcomed each as they arrived, noting who was and was not present. Those who came were some who would not be expected, unless one knew their pasts.

Just being in the West implied some semblance of strength and ability. Some were here by choice, some not so much choice. But they all were here now, in this place, with the same bond...they were tired of living under Barker. Each had been used or abused or belittled in some way and had reached a point inside where it just couldn't go on.

Kerner noted the shopkeepers, the doctor, the blacksmith and his son, as well as more than one lady of the night.

"Ok, I asked you all here because I knew you'all weren't keen on this man Barker and most of ya's has suffered in some way. We been quiet and 'bidin' our time, but I can't stomach this no more. Barker's gone after this Jinker fella, but he ain't gonna stop there. He wants the Gruber ranch and this'll be a perfect chance. I think he intends to kill Grace and Luke."

There was a gasp amidst the group.

"If he does, we'll see him hang!" One voice cried.

"Even he wouldn't do that!" another said.

A saloon girl came forward. Timidly she spoke. "It's true. One of the men said something to me when...well...said Barker'd do anything to get Grace out of the way. Some of the men want to...mistreat her."

A rumble of disapproval was heard.

"I think we need to go help." It was Kerner. "We can't sit here any longer and keep our dignity. This is our town."

"What do you suggest, Kerner?"

"That we follow Barker's men and they'll lead us to Grace, Luke and the man Jinker. Many of us has experience from the war, so we can flank 'em."

"Some of us is gonna get hurt."

"Likely. But we cain't sit back no mo' an' do nuttin." It was a bearded old man with a scar across his forehead. "I'd ruther die than be a lapdog fer Barker and watch as he hurts women an' chillerns. It'll get worse an' worse. None of us'n's'll be safe. Missus Gruber's a fine lady an Luke is fine as they comes."

There were murmurs of approval.

Kerner spoke. "Ok, we need to meet back here in an hour, saddled and ready. Now, there are three of Barker's men still in town." He looked to the saloon girls. "Emmy, Rita, Dotty – I hate ta ask this, but we need them to be distracted so's we can get out of town without their knowing it. I ain't askin you to…you know…just keep them distracted. Give them drinks. But they'll notice me being gone of'n they go to the saloon." His eyes lingered on Emmy.

The three girls glanced at each other. Emmy, the oldest, smiled. "Oh, we'll take care of them all right. They won't be a bother. We'll do more than distract them." She swirled her hips. "But you all need to understand…you can't fail. Otherwise we're in trouble."

"What about some of the others? Logan, the banker, if'n he finds out, he'll ride to send word to Barker."

There was a ruckus at the edge of the crowd. Two men were holding Mattie Edwards, the wife of the hostler. They brought her forward.

"Found her tryin' ta sneak off."

"She's sweet on one of Barker's men"

"That ain't true!" The woman asserted. Her husband came forward.

"It is true, you worthless woman! Don't you think I have eyes? I been seein' you sneak off into the barn with that gunfighter Carson. He been havin' his way with you."

She looked at him wide-eyed.

"Ok, we gotta gather up any who know we are leaving. Use extreme care. You all know who is and who ain't with us. Rita, can you fix Mrs. Edwards up for a while so she cain't do nothin?"

Rita sidled up and grabbed the woman by the arm. "With pleasure." Quickly one of the other girls tied a bandanna in the woman's mouth so she could not cry out.

"Johnson, Holcomb – I'm asking you to stay here in town, gather up anyone who seems suspicious. Keep very alert. Get Logan if'n he even glances sideways. Keep them in that barn back of the store. Truss 'em good. Take a roll of hemp from the store." The men nodded and hurried away.

132

An hour later, a group of fifteen armed and grim-faced riders quietly led their horses for a half-mile before mounting. It was dusk.

Chapter 16

Grace led them swiftly into the hills. She wanted to put as much distance between them and the sure-to-come pursuit as possible. She knew Barker would be undaunted in trying to catch up. After all, it would be an opportunity to eliminate them all. For all her youth, she read the situation for what it was.

She remembered her father speak of a trail high up on the ridges that had several lookout points. If they could get that far they could camp out and maybe would not be found.

It was hard for her to think that her father and grandfather had bad blood between them. She did not understand it all, but had seen a change in her father after her mother died. It's like he started to see the ranch again. He quit looking for more and sought to improve what he had. He had become more attentive to her, teaching her deliberately the ways of the ranch and the ways of the men and women of the West.

He had taken her to town once, where she saw a pretty woman walking the street with a parasol. Her father had mused to her about how at night anything could happen, but during the day and on the street like this the woman was treated like a lady. It was the way of the West. He had also mentioned to her that you never knew the past of many of the people. This particular woman had survived a near massacre and was an expert shot. It was the same with many, he said. Many of the men had trapped, fought Indians or been in the war. The fact that they wore aprons now or maybe even were drunk half the time didn't change the story of their past. He had taught her that a person's past was but part of the story. What was written in the present and the future was what would be remembered. Men and women learned and changed and grew through the years. At least the smart ones did.

She'd wondered since whether he was referring to others or to himself.

It was late afternoon when they saw dust several miles back. They were followed! They needed to keep moving, but their horses were tired. She knew that the men coming would eventually need to rest their horses also, so she took the time to rest for a half hour. They were into the hills now, so their dust would be less visible. It would also be slower going.

She was glad to have Jinker along. The man was solid and very skilled with a gun. If they had to hole up, he would be a valuable asset with his rifle. She was also a good shot, but her 1873 Trapdoor Springfield would not be as fast as the Henry. But she would try and make every shot count. The hands at the ranch, before they were murdered or run off, had taught her well.

Luke could shoot, but was not big enough to handle a rifle. Before leaving the ranch house, she had given him an old pepperbox pistol that he had proudly stuck in his belt. She had reminded him that he must brace himself, since it was not unknown for flash to set off other barrels.

As she stood with Jinker and Luke, peering into the distance, she glanced at Jinker. He looked back at her with concern.

"What is it, Jinker?"

"Missus Grace, I done got's a bad feelin' 'bout dis. Dey's a lot of riders comin.'"

"Lem will find us."

"Mebbe, but he don' know where we uns is. Dem riders gonna be here long afore him. We's outnumbered by a lot. You's got some place in mind fer us to go?"

"I figured we could lose them in the hills." She looked doubtful. Jinker looked into the distance.

"We's got's to go where we might find help. We's may not make it today, but if'n we's keep goin' in da night…"

"Jinker, you have something on your mind."

"Yes'm. How fer to your grandpappy's?"

"I don't know. It's a good days ride, likely."

"We got's to go somewheres. Dey's gonna trap us up here."

"I do not know my grandfather nor do I know that he has any interest in helping me."

"Well, missus Grace, I jus' don' see how's we can do dis' and make it. Mebbe if'n I stay here an' distract 'em, den you's and Luke can head dat way."

"They'd kill you."

"Well, ma'am, yes'm dey would. But I sho' cain't tink of no other way. We need help."

Grace stared into the distance. She appeared to resolve confusion in her mind and stuck out her chin. "We'll head towards the mountains. I'm not sure if my grandfather will help, but I guess we need to give him the chance. At the least, we may run into some of his outriders."

They mounted and worked their way back behind the next ridge and headed toward the notch in the distant mountains where she heard her grandfather lived.

Just before rounding the ridge, Grace glanced back and noted that the dust cloud was closer than before. She urged her horse onward.

Teague, Grizzard and the men rode hard the next morning. All were hardened and honed by the experiences of life and war and the frontier. None of those situations gave any quarter to weakness and questioning.

Skerby had shown up at the last minute and, with a glare between he and Grizzard, fell in with the men.

Mid morning they took a break to rest the horses. As they did so, Teague and Grizzard walked off a ways together.

Teague cleared his throat. "Mind if I ask a question?"

"Ask all you want. I like you, Preacher. I think you and I might understand each other. Life has not turned out for either of us the way we planned. So ask away. You may or may not get an answer."

"You built this ranch far from any town. Your men keep to themselves. They seem to need no one but each other. I'm curious."

Grizzard paused, scanning the horizon. "Preacher, the war changed many of us. There was enough bloodshed and pain for ten lifetimes. My men and I went through a lot together. After the war we wanted nothing but to be left alone, to have peace. I have to admit that there were some instances of tragic brutality that were required of my men. It changed us. So, after the war, about thirty of us came west. Only three of us were married. We found this place in the mountains where we thought we'd be left alone. We built a life here. Yes, I'm still the one in charge – or at least the one they look to. They call me Colonel at times. Yet each man here is his own man. A few have left and, strangely enough, others from our regiment have found us. We have a deep bond. Some have taken wives and brought them here. Some of the wives had their own reasons for seeking this solitude. A couple found they couldn't handle it and left. It is our way of life, and I can tell you that to head to battle again is only out of necessity. Each man was handpicked for this, but had the right to refuse without any questions asked. They know what they are doing, and are prepared to do whatever is necessary. They know that we will face tough men; they know they may be hurt; they know they may die. But they ride today for each other and for Grace and Luke." He glanced around. "Each man here but Moose has at least one child of his own. They understand."

They turned to go to their horses, but Grizzard paused and looked at Teague. "Allow me the return gesture of a question."

"Sure."

"I know some things about you. I went back to St. Louis a couple years ago and was talking to a friend and he mentioned a tragic incident. Well…enough said of that. Have you had any success in, shall we say, taking care of details?"

The man also known as Preacher paused. "Yes, some of the details are taken care of. There is another man I need to find. He was the leader. As it is, I have been unable to locate him nor do I have any leads."

Grizzard turned and looked Preacher full in the face. "Just don't let it destroy your future. Don't miss the opportunity for happiness, Preacher. Though it seems an impossibility, it is there if you want it. Oftentimes it comes in simplicity and solitude. My men and I have learned that. Maybe that's why I agreed to help. Life is more than the past. I also may add the words of a Frenchman named Victor Hugo who wrote these words while we were at war. 'There is a prospect greater than the sea, and it is the sky; there is a prospect greater than the sky, and it is the human soul.' Take care for that which lies within you, Preacher. For that within you impacts more than this life."

Preacher met the man's gaze. He nodded.

"Colonel!" They both turned their heads.

"What is it, Lewis?"

"Rider coming this way...looks like Peachy." Teague's eyebrows rose at the mention of the man's name. Grizzard noted this and smiled wryly.

"Don't let the handle fool you, Preacher. He got it during the war when he would brave enemy fire to gather peaches from a tree between the lines. A braver man does not exist."

One of the men, Blackie, stepped out beyond the rocks to wave at Peachy, who was headed down a lower trail. Peachy pulled up, reaching for his weapon before he recognized his fellow. He then spurred his horse to the group and dismounted. One of the men took the reins as Peachy approached Grizzard.

"Colonel, they's dust off to the east. Looks like a group of riders, headed to the hills. I'm not sure, but I thought I detected dust in the ridges off Blanner Point. Had to be a small party. Looks like the folks down below on the trail of the riders up top. I used the glass, but they's a bit far away yet. But it looks as if the group up top is three riders, one of them a child."

Grizzard looked to Preacher. "Looks like I may meet my grandson sooner than planned. Peachy?"

"Colonel?"

"What's your guess on where the small party is headed?"

"Looks like they's headed roundabout but thisaway. A mite higher than us."

Preacher spoke, "Looks like they are coming to you for help."

"Mount up, let's ride with a purpose men. Keep your eyes open."

Chapter 17

"Missus Grace, we got's to rest dese hosses."

Grace pulled up. "We've got to stay ahead of Barker's men, Jinker." Jinker noted she was flustered, struggling to deal with the situation. It was a trial for someone her age.

"Dey's pushin' as hard as us, Missus Grace. Dey's gonna hafta rest, too." He caught her eye and gave a slight tilt of his head towards Luke. The boy was swaying in the saddle, worn out. She nodded back at Jinker.

"Let's take a few minutes to rest and stretch our legs then. Jinker, can you go back a bit and see how close Barker's men are?"

"Yes'm ."

Before he left, he helped Luke to the ground. The boy walked to the side of the trail and sat down against a rock and fell asleep almost instantly.

Looking at her brother, Grace faced the reality of her life. Neither one of them had ever thought it would come to this. Both parents dead, running for their lives and trying to reach a grandfather whom she didn't know and who likely hated them. And where was Lem? He would do anything to help, and was very capable of doing so, but Barker had a lot of men. She found herself thinking of Lem, of his strength, his confidence, even of the pain she glimpsed in his eyes every so often. She was drawn to him.

She remembered talking to him over a meal when he first arrived at the ranch. He spoke of how many will hope for the best when tough times arrive, which amounts to little preparation, whereas others will prepare for the worst. She realized now was the time to prepare for the worst. They must find a place suitable to make a stand.

"Missus Grace!" It was Jinker, hurrying back. "We got's a bad problem! Dat one group what is down below is gettin' close, but dey's worse den dat. Deys 'nother bunch comin' from high and b'hind. We got's to ride. We got's to find a place to hole up. We got's to pick a spot! I'se gonna take the lead." He went to Luke and shook his shoulder. "Luke, you come b'hind me an' Missus Grace you follow close."

143

Grace's heart leapt. There was a sort of despair within her, yet a determination, a hardness she was unused to. She had two people whose lives were in her hands. Luke could do little and they needed to protect him. She had no doubts that Barker would try his best to have her and Luke "accidentally" killed in the crossfire of a gun battle. She would fight to the end to foil his plans and to take Barker out! She was backed into a corner. She remembered being told years ago that there were few things more dangerous than a wildcat or a man backed into a corner. Well, she was backed into a corner.

"Is you able to hang on a bit more, Luke?"

"Yes, Jinker." He was obviously about all in.

"Let's ride, Jinker! We'll go as far as we can. Keep a look out for a place to make a stand!"

They spurred their horses.

Barker pulled up. His outrider was approaching.

"Mr. Barker, they's up there. 'Bout a mile or so. They's heading into the rough high ground."

Barker smiled. "Looking to find a hole to make a fight, I expect. Exactly what we want. Men! We want that mulatto for murder! A hundred dollars for the man that gets him! Carson!"

"Yes, boss?" Barker led him aside. He spoke to the gunman in a whisper.

"You have taken my wages and now it's time for you to earn it." He glanced at the hills and then at the other men, assuring himself that they were out of earshot. "It'll be very beneficial if nobody lives. If it happens that some are killed in the crossfire, no questions will be asked. They are aiding in the escape of a criminal. Am I understood?"

"You want the girl and the boy dead."

Barker winced. "It must be accidental – he accentuated the last word. I don't trust these lamebrains, but I think you and I understand each other and that you have the skills needed for this…situation."

"Ok, but it'll cost you five hundred extra."

Barker glared at him. "Why the extra?"

"Because I'll need to leave the country if anybody gets to wondering. Takes a bit of cash to make a new name."

"You got it."

Jinker was looking around desperately. They were almost out of time and they needed a hole. He spied a narrow chute between some boulders and called to Grace and Luke to follow. Grace had gladly turned this search over to Jinker. He would know best, having been a soldier.

They came to the top of a little outcropping with a sort of walled in area of a quarter acre.

There was protection for the horses. Grace helped Luke down. Jinker looked swiftly around.

The rocks formed a rough circle. There were a couple higher areas allowing a view over the mountainside. There were scattered boulders around, with some leaning against others and forming natural shelters.

"Luke, git on over der an' git in dat hole in dem rocks. Keep yo head down. Missus Grace, you ever shoot a man?"

"No."

"Well, you got's to git over any hesitation, 'cause dis is da time when we'uns got's to unnerstand dat dey's gonna try and kill us." He looked over at the boy and whispered to Grace, "Dey's gonna kill Luke. We got's to kill dem first, and keep dem away as long as we can. We got's to hope dat dey's gonna be help a'comin', dat somebody's gonna hear da shootin'."

Grace looked at him fiercely. "I will kill as many as I can. Where do you want me?"

"Over dere, by dem rocks. Dey's gonna try an git through dat notch. You stop 'em! I'se over here, an' I'll watch dese two approaches. Make every shot count. Wait till dey really shows deyself's. Don't show no more of yourself dan you's got's to. Don' make no target."

Grace looked around. Jinker waved her over to the high point where they could both look back along the mountain. He pointed and she saw the dust cloud, now close. He suddenly touched

146

her shoulder and pointed. Another dust cloud further up the mountain! Two groups coming for them! Her heart sunk, and Jinker looked at her.

"Dis is it, Missus Grace. We got's to fight for our lives. An' specially for Luke." She saw him glance to the sky, then over her shoulder. He squinted.

"Dey's more dust!" He rushed across to the other side and climbed partly up to get a better look. "Missus Grace, I ain't sure, but I don' think dey's part of Barker's group. Dey's comin' directly from the mountains. Dat may be jus' what we been hopin' fer. You 'spose Len done got Grizzard comin? Too fer to tell yet, but I swear dey's a big hoss in dat bunch." He looked at Grace. "We got's to fight with hope! It gonna be hard, and you may git shot. Ya got's ta keep fightin.' Unnerstand me?"

She nodded, and Jinker saw a fierce determination in her eyes. They both turned as a bullet struck a rock nearby.

As they rode the trail towards Grace and Luke, Preacher suddenly pulled his horse to a halt, and pointed along the ridge. The others reined their horses close.

"There's another party coming from behind! Two parties converging on them. I haven't seen any dust for a few minutes with Grace. Jinker's found them a hole."

147

They heard the faint sound of gunfire beginning. Still about three miles away, they knew they needed to move quickly.

Grizzard looked stern and turned to his men. "Darter, Hoke, Blackie come with us. Lewis, Peachy, Moose take the high point and see if you can come in from behind that other bunch and give them something to write to momma about."

"For the wages of sin is death." The others turned to Preacher. He urged Rex on. The horse seemed to understand the urgency.

The groups split and they began picking their way through the rocks as quickly as they could. The trail wound with the terrain and there was much doubling back. As they drew closer they could hear answering gunfire from Grace and Jinker. Preacher recognized the sound of Jinker's Henry and knew that Grace had a trapdoor Springfield. There was a part of him that was calm, knowing Jinker was there, but there was part of him that was bordering on panic for Grace and Luke. He found himself wondering about his feelings. Despite his internal wall, he found himself caring for this young lady.

He heard another gun go off and smiled. It was the sound of a trapdoor Springfield. Grace was fighting! He urged Rex onward.

Jinker reminded Luke to stay down as more shots came their way. Searching fire. Luke hunkered into the hole and Jinker settled in, glancing at Grace to be sure she was set.

A head showed between two boulders, but Grace let it go unchallenged. She knew they would be baiting her, trying to find her location. There was no shot, and the man climbed quickly over the boulders and crouched, scanning the rocks. Grace slowly drew a bead on the man, let out her breath and fired. The man flew backwards against the rocks. Blood poured over his shirtfront as he died.

Grace paled at the sight, but knew she had no choice. Instantly there were bullets whizzing by and slapping rocks. She ducked down but kept her eyes on the gap in the rocks. She scanned the area, knowing they would try to find another point of entrance. None would be eager to use the one where the man died. She looked towards Jinker, and saw him glance quickly her way and give her a nod. She saw him bring his gun to his shoulder for a quick shot, and heard a man scream.

The shots became almost continuous, as Barker's men sought to gain hits by chance ricochets. Jinker and Grace lay hunkered. Grace turned her head to see blood running down Jinker's face. Eyes wide, she realized it was superficial, as he smiled and gestured.

Grace realized there was no way out, unless help came quickly. Otherwise, the best they could do was to take as many as they could of

Barker's men with them as they died. She had no time for regrets, just a realization of the truth, and it made her burn with anger, especially for Luke. A couple of bullets had ricocheted close to him and he was crying with his hands over his face. Seeing a man peer through a gap, she fired again, saw his face disappear as rock shards blasted his eyes. He'd be out of it.

Yet that didn't matter, because it was just a matter of time before they closed in. They could not count on the party from behind either being help or even getting here on time. All they had to do was hit she or Jinker and one person could not defend this position. She realized she was bleeding from fragment skin wounds. And she was crying. And she was fighting for her life!

Outside the position, Carson listened intently for the sound of the rifle he'd identified as Grace's. He was trying to peg her location. As she fired again, he shifted his head and smiled. She was over to the left. He began to work his way over, being careful not to get shot by Barker's men. He waved at Barker, who signaled for the men in one area to cease fire, giving Carson a chance to work closer. He peered slowly around boulders as he crept forward.

Grace noted that the shooting had stopped on one side. She looked at Jinker, who also had noted it and was looking, brow furrowed, in her direction. They both realized something was up, that Barker's men had some sort of plan. Jinker had to return to his watch, as men were closing in on his side also. He turned and fired as a man rose up before him, blowing the man backward.

As Grace looked around, she thought she saw movement past a narrow crack. So that was it! A man was slowly working his way up. She turned her gun to where she anticipated the man would be.

Chapter 18

Carson saw a flash of color as he went by the small crack, and realized he may have been seen. He waited a moment and turned around to peer carefully through the crack close to the ground. There! It was Grace, and she was looking ahead to where he would have been if he continued. He wasn't sure if he could get a good shot through the crack, but looked up and realized there was a notch towards the top of the formation. If he could just inch up there and surprise her. Just a quick shot would be enough. He began to inch his way carefully up.

Over the top of the ridge there was an increase in gunfire. He paused, wondering. Then he heard someone holler, "Someone else is here!"

He quickly inched upward until he could peer over the rock. There! It was Grace Gruber, and she was looking the other way. Grinning, he brought his pistol up, thumbing the hammer back as he did so. Taking careful aim at Grace, he pulled the trigger.

She was looking backwards where she had heard some shouts, trying to fathom what was going on. Just then Luke screamed, she turned quickly and at that moment a bullet marked the rock where her head was just moments before. She ducked and came up a few feet to the left and saw a man's head over the rock. Firing, she missed, but the man disappeared. She recognized him as the gunman that was always with Barker. She reloaded. Her father had taught her well, spending time practicing both shooting and loading. He had told her the need to load quickly but carefully. She remembered his words:

"Grace, it won't do any good to shoot one shot but get killed because you can't get the next shot loaded. At the same time, you can't rush, because you'll fumble and have to start over. All of this with someone shooting at you." He had forced her to practice loading over and over till her finger hurt and her arms and shoulders ached. Luckily she had a carbine version, with the shorter barrel. She had practiced until she could reliably load ten times a minute. She remembers her father's smile and nod of praise. Well, that practice had never been tested, but it was paying off now.

She turned to Luke, who was pointing. Unable to see where he was pointing, she was about to move when she heard a boot scuff a rock to her right and turned in time to put a bullet in a man about to get behind her. As she reloaded, she heard Luke scream and turned in absolute panic as she heard the pepperbox go off – all barrels – and saw two men drop mere feet from her brother. Neither moved.

The man known as Teague and also as Preacher was angry, seething inside that men like Barker would take advantage of women and children. He came through the rocks at a crouching run and, seeing the gunslinger Carson climbing, levered a shot that came close but served only to cause the man to drop instantly to the ground and crouch behind the rocks.

Gunfire was everywhere, and he came to the gap in the rocks that was the death of one man, noting the body with a shot to the heart.

"Grace!"

Grace heard the yell, recognized it and turned to the gap.

"Lem!"

"I'm coming in!"

Carefully, he peered around the corner, revealed himself, to see Grace with a bead on him. Recognition came to her face and she lowered the gun, then raised it again and shot to his left. He crawled in, seeing Jinker turn suddenly and fall, wounded. Jinker looked at Teague with desperation on his face. He'd taken one through the shoulder. Suddenly Peachy and Moose were beside him, restraining him. Teague saw their mouths move as they spoke to Jinker to reassure him they were there to help, then let him go. Grace jumped, but he assured her they were friends. Moose slipped an arm under the mulatto to help him stand. Peachy swung his pistol back and forth, watching for Barker's men. Teague grabbed Luke and they all slipped out of the wall of rocks towards where one of Grizzard's men was guarding the horses a couple hundred yards away. They fled down a small game trail. Teague looked around. The attackers were occupied elsewhere with Grizzard's men. Suddenly the shooting stopped completely as Barker yelled.

At that moment, Old Man Grizzard and another, the man named Hoke, came in leading horses. Grizzard reached for Luke, but the boy cowered back against Teague. Tears had left rivulets down his face as they coursed through the dust. He had a deep fear in his eyes.

"It's ok, Luke, go with him." Luke glance back then grabbed Grizzard's arm. Grizzard mounted quickly and drew Luke up with him. A shot rang out and Grizzard grunted and leaned over, a look of pain on his face. Then, he recovered and wrapped his arms around Luke and rode through the boulders, hunched in the saddle.

Hoke did the same thing with Grace, throwing her before him in the saddle to protect her, and began to weave amongst the boulders after Grizzard.

"Can you walk, Jinker?"

"If'n I got's to." He turned as he heard a swish in the sand and levered a shot. At the same moment Teague let loose of Jinker and, red-faced, began to approach the rock behind which the firing had come. When the faces appeared again, he shot both shooters and, trembling with rage, turned to grab Jinker and they moved away. The mulatto could feel the rage in the man.

Chapter 19

All around the rock formation, chaos was rampant. Barker's men, confident in their attack, suddenly found themselves on the receiving end. Men were down and others were huddled in the rocks. They were no match for Grizzard's battle hardened and savvy soldiers. And to Barker's disadvantage, he had drawn enough unfamiliar men to this journey that even his own hands could not tell who was who. More than one of his men went down with a bullet from someone who had been horseback with him earlier.

Barker was wide-eyed with confusion as he searched the rocks for a target. He turned as Carson crawled desperately through the rocks and swung beside him. Carson instantly realized how close he had come to being shot, as Barker's pistol stared him in the face. Slowly Barker lowered his gun.

"Boss, we gotta get outa here."

"Who's out there?"

"I'm not sure, but someone is attacking us."

"There are idiots shooting at anything that moves. Let's get back." Barker turned and crawled back through the rocks towards the trees in the distance where they had tied their horses. They'd gone only a few feet when they rounded a boulder and found a man staring wide-eyed at the sky, a hole drilled neatly in his forehead. Barker swore and nervously stepped over the body and went on.

After creating the chaos, Grizzard's other men faded back and met at their rally point. As they filtered in, each took stock of the others and noted Darter and Peachy wearing bloody bandages but ok. All eyes turned as Old Man Grizzard audibly groaned as he lowered Luke to the ground. They noticed the blood dripping down his saddle. The men rushed to him and noticed he had caught one low and hard.

"Lewis! Help me bind this up quick. We've got to get out of here." They helped him from the saddle. He was pale and struggling, but they'd never known the man to give up, and he wasn't doing so now.

Grace spoke. "Who is this man? And who are you?"

Lewis looked over his shoulder. "He's your grandfather." Grace's eyes widened and her hand went to her mouth. Luke turned and looked at the man and then looked at Grace.

"How did you know we were here?"

Grizzard looked up at her. "Teague came to us and convinced a stubborn old man that there was some responsibility left in my life. You're my kin." He paused. "I'm sorry it took so long for me to come to my senses. I should have come to help a lot sooner. I'm sorry, Luke. I'm sorry, Grace." There was silence as Lewis worked on Grizzard, Grace stared at her grandfather, and the men stared back and forth.

"Where's Lem?"

"He said something about taking care of things."

Moose spoke: "He took his horse. I ain't seen a horse like that nowhere. I reckon he'll ketch up to whatever he's chasin'. But I seen him take a bullet in the leg. It'll slow him after a fashion."

Moose saw the fear in Grace's eyes at the mention of Teague being shot."

Indeed, Rex was running like the wind, covering more ground than the average horse. On his back, Teague was staring intently ahead at a dust cloud a mile or so ahead, grimacing with the pain in his leg. He had wrapped his bandana around the wound, which was just above his knee. Everything worked, but he knew it would be stiff later if he tried to dismount in a hurry. Blood was smeared on his stirrup.

The survivors of Barker's outfit had quickly mounted and left when they noted the firing slow and realized it was over. They scrambled over bodies of their fellow riders, some killed by themselves in the chaos. More than one vomited on the run. They were making an effective escape, as do those who have no leadership and only desire distance. They hung together for safety, but holstered their weapons and rode.

Teague had slipped away earlier once he knew that Grace and Luke were safe. He knew that Rex would eat the distance. The horse loved to run. It had been slower in the rocks, but once they got below the formations, he was able to cover ground.

He was seething! The anger that had been welling up inside him since....well....it was erupting towards this man Barker. How dare he try and push Grace and Luke off their land! How dare he try and get them killed! What kind of a man would do such a thing? A blood lust was building in Teague, his senses intent upon the task ahead of him.

This feeling had been upon him several times now. He would forget all sense of self and all his being focused upon his opponent and stopping the injustice. Ever since...ever since...ever since his world fell apart. Ever since then he had been on the move, seeking, searching for the final move in this chess game. He would see the end of those who destroyed his life.

The dust cloud slowed and stopped ahead. His brow crinkled with questioning. He was so focused he failed to see the flash of color as two riders made their escape further along the slope behind him.

The dust cloud had, indeed, stopped. The frothing horses and wide-eyed men had rounded a bend to find their path blocked by a mob of the folks from town. They had guns and those guns were pointed at McNary and the riders. McNary was riding lead, as Barker and Carson had slipped away. McNary was mad – mad at everything and everybody for what had happened that day. He had seen Barker and Carson go another direction and was cursing Barker as a coward. Now, he was in charge of this group. Before them stood a wall of dismounted men, bristling with gun barrels.

McNary pulled up and the men stopped in a mass, some horses bumping others and one man even thrown from his horse, as the stop was so sudden. He lay, groaning and trying to rise to his knees. He heard a hammer click and chose to stay on the ground.

The man McNary, who walked like a Banty rooster on the ground, did not strut now. He recognized the men from town, and also recognized that there were guns pointed at them. He was aware of the danger, but tried to bluff.

"You townsfolk! Get out of the way and get back to town!" He yelled commandingly, but no one moved.

"We do not listen to you any more, McNary. Drop your guns." It was Kerner.

One of McNary's men cursed the townsfolk, and McNary turned in time to see him draw his gun.

McNary yelled, "No!" But it was too late. The man fired and Kerner dropped. But that was missed as the entire area erupted in gunfire. The townsfolk fired almost as a volley, all their pent up anger being released as they fired into the wildly plunging melee of horsemen. Pitching horses prevented any aim by McNary and his men. The man who shot Kerner flew backwards off his horse as a load of buckshot took him in the chest. Others screamed and fell.

In a few moments it was over. McNary lay face down in the dirt, blood running across the ground. Several others were lifeless and some were groaning. Horses stood panicked or had run off. Two horses lay dying. No man remained on a horse. All of Barker's men were either dead or wounded. Two men afoot were seen in a limping rush back down the trail. One of the men from town ran after them. There were the sounds of a shotgun and the townsman returned – without prisoners.

Among the townsfolk, blessings were recognized that day. Due to the inability of the mounted men to aim as horses plunged and jumped, Kerner was the worst hit. He was hit high in the chest and a couple of the others rushed to him. The blacksmith and a couple others were hit in the arm, but the rest were superficial scratches.

As they took stock of the situation, men rushed into the group of horsemen, disarming and angrily shoving those able to walk into a group. The wounds were grievous and disturbing among the riders, as several of the townsmen had carried shotguns. A couple of them coughed and died as they lay bleeding. It was the first some had seen of such wounds, while for others it brought back memories of the war.

The townsfolk, after the shock of the moment, looked around and began to smile as only those could who had been through a moment facing death and had remained standing. More than one looked at their hats and stuck fingers through the holes, grinning. Then there was laughter, a sort of nervous chuckle, along with others holding back tears.

"Dad gum! We done it!" It was the blacksmith, standing next to his son. "I were sure we'd of had a bunch of us kilt." His son was in shock yet, staring at the pistol in his hand and realizing he also had shot into the men, though unsure if he had hit anything.

One of the others said, "Get these no-goods together and let's get some horses so's we can get back to town."

"Then we can take care of the rest!"

As they moved to round up the men, there was the pounding of hoofs and Teague came round the bend and pulled Rex to a halt as a couple men turned their weapons towards him.

"Don't shoot!"

He dismounted slowly and began to hobble around looking at the men on the ground and the men they were holding. Barker and Carson were not among them!

"Where's Barker and his paid gun Carson?"

The men looked at each other. "He wasn't in the bunch that we corralled here."

The man known in rough times as Preacher was incensed, realizing he had pursued the wrong target and that Barker, and likely Carson, had gotten away. He mounted and rode back up the trail for a ways, then stopped and scanned the ridges and outcroppings above.

He cursed under his breath.

Chapter 20

Back in the hills, the opposite direction from the battle site, Grizzard's men had ridden several miles to a line cabin. When they arrived, one of their men was waiting behind the cabin with Winchester ready, until he recognized his fellow hands.

"Hey, I thought I heerd guns earlier when I was up top. How's come you didn't invite me?"

"Never you mind, Peeper! Jus' help us get the Colonel down. He's been shot."

Hoke had helped Grace down and she rushed to give a hand with her grandfather. As his men eased him down, they pulled aside and, with a glance at each other, let Grace help him to the cabin. They knew that the wound was serious, but they had seen worse.

Entering the cabin, they lowered him to one of the cots. Looking around, he groaned loudly. Lewis glanced at him.

"I know it hurts, boss! We'll get some likker in ya."

"It ain't the wound I'm groanin' about, Lewis! It's this cabin. It stinks like the south end of a northbound bluebelly!" He glanced around. "I got to get up here more often, I guess, or you men'll live like vermin!"

The men turned to each other and smiled. They knew he would fight.

Grace looked at the men and wondered about their looks. She went to the stove and found a pot of coffee, scalding hot. Lewis joined her.

"I'll dump this and get some fresh water if I know where to get it."

"There's a spring a few yards up the hill. You'll see the path. But never mind now. This hot coffee will do fine to clean the wound."

They cleansed the wound, with Grace helping Lewis. All the while watching her grandfather. He was a fine looking man, she thought. She could see the resemblance to her father.

"Grace, I hate for you to see me this way."

"It's ok, grandfather. Just rest and let us fix you up." He smiled and closed his eyes as he grimaced.

166

"Bullet went clean through, Colonel. You've lost a lot of blood, so you'll have to sit and eat and gain weight and be worthless for a spell."

Grizzard glanced at Lewis.

"Thanks for giving it to me straight, Lewis. You know how to make a man feel good." He gave a chuckle but quickly squelched it as he winced. Lewis looked at the men, all gathered and looking at the wounded man. A smile coursed across their faces.

Grizzard looked across the room at Luke who had sideways scooted in the door. He made eye contact and smiled.

"What a fine strapping young man you are, Luke." He glanced over at Lewis. "Lewis, you expect we've got a horse Luke's size to cut out of the herd. Maybe that nice paint with the spots? He'll need something to ride back and forth from his ranch to mine."

Luke was wide-eyed and grinned at his new-found grandfather.

Lewis also grinned. "Yep, I expect that horse'd work nicely."

Jinker was more critical, but it appeared that the bullet had not hit anything vital. Even so, it had not gone all the way through, so Lewis had the men hold him down while he probed the wound and found the bullet. The man was unconscious by the time they were finished.

"Best he be out fer awhile. That was a tough hit."

167

Grace looked worried. "Neither Luke nor I would be alive if it weren't for him. Will he live?"

"With the right care and a lot of rest he stands a chance. No promises."

Grace was already cleansing the superficial wounds of the others, cleansing them also with coffee and some of the liniment that Lewis produced from his saddlebag.

Lewis gave orders.

"Moose! Peachy! Go back down the trail a piece and see if'n there's anything we need to worry 'bout. Hoke, see about something to eat." He walked outside and looked around.

"Somebody get some more water for coffee." Suddenly he furrowed his brow and turned all the way around looking.

"Where's Skerby?"

Having been detailed to watch the horses at the battle, the little man had done so until the men started to return. Then he had slipped off quietly with his horse and picked his way up and to the battle site, avoiding Grizzard's men as they fled. He pulled his LeMat and entered the rock formation. Carefully skirting the rocks, he pieced the battle together by the placement of the dead, who already were attracting flies.

It didn't take long to find the central point where Grace and Jinker had been placed, and then he found where Luke had been, noting the men shot apparently by Luke. He examined the bodies. Musta been a pepperbox. He smiled when he saw no blood in Luke's hiding spot.

He worked his way outwards from that point, cautious for any man still wounded and dangerous. Apparently, though, the men who left had taken the wounded with them. All the men here were either killed outright or died from their wounds – likely from bleeding. He did not miss the man he figured was first shot by Grace. He admired the aim.

At one point he stopped and carefully knelt down, examining marks in the dirt. Two men, and they did not go the same direction as the others. Two men, independent. He followed their tracks further to where the horses had been. The tracks were all jumbled together, but he found where two had gone off towards the top of the ridge while the others grouped and went back down the trail. Following a few yards, he found where the horses had stepped into soft dirt.

Barker! He had noted before that barker's horse towed in and drug his left rear hoof a mite when walking slow. The other horse must be Carson! They had flown the coop.

He had seen Teague in the distance pursuing the other group, no doubt seeking Barker. Well, he wasn't going to find them because they had fled another way.

Skerby grinned and began to walk his horse slowly after Barker's tracks.

Teague walked his horse back to the towns-folk.

"Mr. Teague?" It was the doctor. He was carrying a bag and had liberal smears of blood on his front. Teague looked at him. It seemed that he was a bit blurry in his vision…

A couple others helped the doctor lower Teague from his horse. He was unconscious.

"This man's lost a mite of blood. So many men think they're tough and then they realize it just takes a loss of blood and they're weak as a child." Slicing the trouser leg, he looked at both sides of the wound, satisfied that the bullet went clear through. Blood still ran from both sides, helping to cleanse it. He poured whiskey through the wound and bound it.

Skerby followed the tracks, being careful not to forsake the fact that the two men might set a trap for him if they realized they were followed. Both were smart men. However, right now they both were likely making a point of getting as far away as possible. It didn't matter if they were followed, as they still had to make distance.

Stopping behind a tall outcropping, he dismounted and peered around. He spotted movement and ducked back behind the rock. He didn't think he'd been seen, but doubt was one of the attitudes that helped keep people alive over the years. He waited a long while before he carefully examined the ridge ahead, saw nothing, and moved out. After carefully watching he approached the ridge itself and, leaving his horse, crawled to the crest and took off his hat to peer over. He did not want to skyline himself.

There! A couple miles ahead were two riders.

Where were they headed? They were going deeper into the mountains. Not a good thing this time of year, what with the snows coming early at the higher elevations. He had known of men who stayed up in the mountains just a few hours too long and never came out.

Wait! There was an old settlement up on the mountain. He remembered going there twenty years ago. Just a handful of buildings, one of them he recalled being of logs. Yet, that must be where they were headed, as they seemed to be traveling with a purpose, almost a beeline.

He looked at the sky. Well, he knew where they were, and likely they would stay there for a while. Else they would not go this deep into the mountains. They probably intended to let things quiet down then slip out of the country. He'd just sort of meander around and come in the back way, just to see where they settle. After all, he had nothing better to do.

Carson had been upset. He was not into running and thought, when they left the battle, that they would circle and head back to town. Instead, Barker was heading into the hills.

"Where'r we headed?"

"Little settlement up yonder in the hills. Abandoned. Be a place to let things cool off."

"Why not just head into town and take care of things?"

Barker, for all his devious nature and his lack of concern for others, had a deep caring for himself. He was also realistic. He sensed that his plans had gone awry. He had seen a dust cloud in front of his men escaping to town. He had a hunch that they had run into trouble. The only thing it could be would be a group from town, as he had not left enough men behind to create so much dust. He was frustrated, but he was alive and unhurt, and had a significant amount of gold on his person. This scheme had failed, but he would live to try again. He was angry inside. He also knew he might sometime sneak back into that town and get more gold he had stashed in a very safe spot under some floorboards in his room. But, best to be alive. He also was aware that Carson was dangerous, especially in his anger and confusion. He must be careful. The man had no loyalty beyond his paymaster. Yet, for all the danger and mistrust, he still needed the man. There was a sense of comfort in having another gun around at times like this.

"I don't think you are aware of all that has happened, Carson. We were hit by another force from who knows where. It was likely Teague's doing, and I think that we are likely the only ones not corralled in some way – or dead."

"I ain't no coward!"

"I'm not saying that. I'm saying that we need to let things calm a little. There are too many of them. In fact, the best thing we can do is sit tight and when it calms and nobody is actively looking for us we slip down out of the hills and out of the country."

"So…we're just going to sit out here and hide, then tuck our tails and run?"

"Yep."

"Well, I don't think I'm going to join you in this journey."

"Up to you. I can keep the gold."

Carson's eyes grew large. "Gold? What gold?"

Barker knew he had the man now, but also realized the danger involved. Many men of even deep loyalty were changed by gold fever. Carson was a paid loyalty, which was pretty low on the totem pole. Yet, if this was worked properly, they would both benefit. He actually knew of no gold, but if he could keep the myth alive in Carson… He had heard from some old drunk about a settlement up here in the deep mountains.

"Story has it that there was a miner in the bunch at the settlement, and that he went out one day and found a vein of gold bigger around than his wrist…"

Chapter 21

Teague lay abed in the hotel for several days, chomping at the bit and realizing that Barker's trail had gone cold. There had been a torrential rain and there was no way to locate the men.

After five days, Grace returned from the mountains and was at Teague's bedside when he awoke from an afternoon's doze. He looked up and saw a look he had not seen for several years. It was a look that could only be deep love. He looked at her, and looked longer. She reached down and put her hand over his. He did not resist nor move away. Nor, however, did he curl his fingers around hers. She patted his hand, pursed her lips and clasped her hands together. Where she wanted him to respond, he was as yet unable.

"I want to thank you, Lem. For all that you have done for me. And how much you mean to me…and Luke." She seemed uncomfortable with this moment, a moment that she wanted to be warm, but was cold.

"What happened to all the men they caught?"

"Those that lived were sent packing with only the clothes on their backs. Warned to never be seen here again."

He looked to the window, which was closed to the chill.

"Kerner?"

"Oh, he'll live and his life will never be the same." She chuckled, despite her feelings. "He's like a hero to these people. He's still abed, but they are lined up to make a pilgrimage to his bedside. Emmy's sticking pretty close."

Teague smiled. "Grizzard?"

"He's a tough man, my grandfather. He'll be fine. And he's been very kind to us, sending some of his men to gather our cattle and work around the place. He sent word that he would enjoy a visit from both myself and Luke in a couple weeks"

"Barker?"

"No sign of him. Lem, maybe you should let sleeping dogs lie."

"You may be right. He's already whipped. His kind are always defeated in the end. I think we clipped his feathers pretty good. Carson I will have to face sometime. His type cannot give up the opportunity to see who is fastest. It's like an obsession with him…I could see it in his eyes. Somewhere he will crop up."

"Lem…?" He saw the look in her eyes again, her yearning and desire for him to respond.

"Grace, I cannot stay. There is a man I must find."

"The last man who killed your wife and son?"

He startled and looked at her, wide-eyed.

"How did you know?"

"I made Jinker tell me."

Teague looked out the window. She watched as his thoughts suddenly were far, far away. She knew she could never have this man when he was divided in his heart. He would not be whole until he had resolved this tragedy. Despite all her feelings and hopes, this man could not be hers…or anybody's…yet.

"I know you got it to do, Lem. I just hope…well…I think you know what I hope." She curled her hand around his and then let it go.

He nodded at her and then turned to the window. She slipped softly out the door.

When the door closed, his head turned towards it and a tear coursed down his cheek.

It was a week later and he had been walking around town gingerly. Many of the townsfolk greeted him with smiles and kind words. Such a difference from before! The fear and intimidation were no longer.

176

One afternoon he decided he would visit Kerner, who had been placed in one of the hotel rooms. He asked the clerk first if it was ok, and the clerk smiled.

"He's been askin' about you, Mr. Teague. I 'spect it's more than fine for you to visit."

Climbing the stairs slowly, he went down the hall and knocked lightly. The door opened and a woman he recognized as serving drinks at the saloon grinned at him. She quickly pulled her dress over her shoulders. This must be Emmy.

"Mr. Teague! Well, please come in." She stepped aside. He noticed her flushed cheeks.

Kerner looked up at him.

"Teague! I'm glad you're here." He noticed the lipstick smeared around the man's mouth. Glancing at Emmy, he saw her grin and look at Kerner. Then she went to the other side of the bed and, with a little hesitation, clasped Kerner's hand and held it.

"Teague, Emmy and I are going to be married."

"That's wonderful! You'll make a nice couple." Emmy and Kerner grinned at each other and squeezed each others' hands. "You've become quite a hero around here, Kerner."

The man looked embarrassed. "Yes, I 'spect so. You know, Teague, it's the first time I've ever felt like I meant something, and the first time I've ever been so happy."

"You deserve it."

Kerner frowned. "Teague, I've got something to show you, and I ain't sure if'n I want to."

Teague's brow furrowed. "What is it?"

Reaching under his pillow, he pulled out a folded sheet of paper. "I was curious and sent a wire to a friend down the line. This is what I got back." He slowly handed it to Teague.

Opening the paper, he scanned the contents. His brow furrowed and a distant look came across his face mixed with a determination and the look of...death. Dropping the paper, he walked out.

The paper lay on the bed.

BARKER NOT HIS REAL NAME STOP OTHER PRISONER HERE SAID HE TALKED ONE NIGHT WHEN DRUNK OF CHANGING HIS NAME BECAUSE OF PEOPLE KILLED IN ROBBERY IN ST. LOUIS

"What was all that about, love?"

"Emmy, the story is that Teague –Preacher – well, his wife and kids were killed in a robbery in St. Louis. He's been after the men for years, found all but one. I think he's seen the last one...and now the man is gone. It was Barker."

Chapter 22

Teague was shocked. Barker! Barker was the last one. He had had him within his grasp and didn't even know it!

He didn't quite know what to do. He did not know where Barker went, but he knew he was not here. Going directly to his room, he began to pack what he had with him. The rest was at the ranch. He then went to the livery where Rex was growing fat and lazy, saddled up and paid his bill.

Mounting slowly, he turned and headed out towards the ranch. He would get his gear and take off. He dreaded facing Grace again, but this was something he needed to do. He was already feeling the rage build up inside. Would he ever be free from it and able to settle again in one place? That was an unknown, but right now it didn't matter. What mattered to his heart right now was finding Barker and clearing the slate.

The weather was crisp. He would need his sheepskin coat before long.

An hour later he cantered into the ranch yard. Luke was out splitting kindling with a hatchet, his breath showing as he exerted himself. He stopped and carefully set the hatchet into the chopping log and ran to greet his friend.

"Hello, Lem!"

"Hey, Luke!"

"Are you feeling better? The leg ok?"

"The leg is doing fine. Just a mite stiff."

The door opened and Jinker slowly walked out. His left arm was in a sling and his chest showed the bulk of a bandage. He still looked a bit weak.

"How you doing, Jinker?"

"Much better, Teague. I'se a bit tired still, but I's pleased to be lookin' at you an' not pushing up daisies back in dem high mountain meadows!" He squinted at Teague. "You got's sumpin' on yer mind. What's ailin' ya?"

"I came to get my gear. I'm heading out."

"Lawd have mercy, Teague. You's barely healed!"

"Doesn't matter. I've got to go."

Jinker had walked over to the horse and looked up. He spoke in a low voice. "Ya found out sumpin' about the last man, I kin tell."

"It was Barker."

"Barker!"

180

"I'm going to see if I can cut his trail somehow."

"But the varmint could be anywheres by now!"

"I know, but…" His eyes looked to the hills and he looked troubled.

"I ain't healed enough to come along. I want ya to know I'd be wit ya if'n I was ready."

"I know you would, Jinker."

"You best get a bait of grub in ya, 'fore ya take yer leave."

Teague looked to the house. Grace was coming out of the door, flour on her apron. She looked at Lem, a look of mixed hurt and yearning.

"I don't know if that's best."

Jinker looked at Grace, then back to Teague.

"I 'tink dey's somethin' here fer you, Lem. She's a fine lady."

"I can't even think of that, Jinker. At least not till…"

"I know…" He looked to Grace and spoke. "I found out Barker was…he was…he killed my wife…and my son. I've got to find him."

She looked at him. Then she walked off the porch and over to his horse. Jinker backed away as Grace spoke in a whisper.

"I know you've got to find him." She ran her hand along the rifle scabbard. Then she looked him in the eyes and spoke, a fire in every word. "And when you find him I want you to kill him

181

like the dirty dog he is!" She almost hissed the last words. Then she reached up and touched his arm. "It's ok, Lem, for you to go. You'd never be really here if you knew the man was still loose. But I really want you to have a good meal before you go. And I'll pack you a bait of grub for the road. Please?"

He looked at her, a yearning in his eyes, a desire to stay, yet a need to go. His hand slipped to hers. He was quiet a moment, his thumb moving in small circles over the top of her hand. She was looking at him, and he could tell she was fighting tears.

"What's for lunch?"

She smiled as she hesitantly pulled away. She knew she had to...for now. She couldn't cage the man. He needed to complete the tasks in his heart. They scared her, but she understood. She wanted a whole man, not half a man. She brushed her hair out of her face.

"Beef stew and the biggest biscuits you've ever seen. 'Bout a half hour...plenty of time for you to get what you need together. Mind you, Lem Teague, only take what you need. I don't mind you leaving things here. Just don't leave them too long." She turned and, with more swish to her hips than he thought necessary, went into the house.

As they sat to eat, Lem reflected briefly as he wiped his spectacles. The four sat together, old friends now, bonded by adversity. Grace, more of a woman than she was months ago, hardened and seasoned with the struggles, yet so feminine. She was, indeed, no longer a child, but a woman. Luke had grown, had experienced what few others his age would, and he was also wiser and saw the true ways of man. He had shot his first men, and that always changed someone. Jinker Jackson…Lem had watched as he casually walked into the house to eat, with no hesitation as in other parts of the country. He had found a home, and Teague did not want to take him away from this. In a way, he was glad that Jinker was not healed, for he was here for Grace and Luke, a capable hand.

As they had grown accustomed when together, they bowed their heads and said a quiet prayer, then a communal amen.

He reached for the biscuits.

"Hello the house!" Teague was up instantly, his pistol in hand. Jinker reached for his rifle, though he'd be unable to handle it. Teague walked to the door and looked out.

Skerby! A bit bedraggled and worn, and likely a mite gamey. He looked as if he had been out in the hills a while.

"Skerby! Why you old Cayuse! There's a few been wondering where you wandered off to. Nobody saw you among the dead or the living after the battle on the mountain."

Skerby sniffed the air. "Whatever I'm sniffin' smells better'n I do. 'Spose there's a mite for a guest?

Grace slipped sideways out the door to see who this was. Her hand purposely brushed Teague's lower back and paused there for a moment. Her eyebrows lifted as she saw the man.

"Who is this, Lem?"

"This is Skerby. He met me on the mountain and showed me the way to your grandfather's. Nothin' but a troublemaker!" He grinned at Grace and she quickly turned to Skerby.

"Light and set, Mr. Skerby. Looks like you could do with a good meal. Wash off around the corner and come in. Luke! See to this man's horse, please. Looks like they've come a long ways." Luke took the man's reins and walked the horse to the barn.

A while later, they sat again to the table, with an extra chair alongside Jinker. Luke stared at Skerby, every once in a while subtly sniffing the air. This wasn't missed by the gangly man.

"Well, son, I been out in the hills livin' off the land for a mite and I ain't had no cause for a bath, nor any need for one. My horse, he never complained and he smells bad 'nuff hisself!"

They spoke of what was going on in town, how Barker was gone and the town was cleaned up and life had returned to normal.

"How's my brother?"

Teague answered. "I hear tell he's doing well. One of the men came to town last week and stopped by to see me. Said Grizzard's healing well and just as cantankerous, which means he'll be fine."

Grace looked wide-eyed. "You're my grand-father's brother? That makes you my great uncle."

"I reckon."

"How come I've never seen you?"

"Oh, I been hither and yon over the country. I check in onc't a while. I seen you now and then. I just weren't on the best of terms with your parents or my brother."

Grace just stared at him, wondering, but also realizing men have their reasons at times for doing what they do, and that it just was what is was.

"Ma'am, these here biscuits is the best I ever done eaten. Now, I fancy myself a mite of a campfire cook, so I'm interested in your recipe."

"Well, thank you, Skerby! I take a couple scoops of flour, a scoop of fat, a bit over a scoop of milk, a tetch of salt, and a couple dollops of baking powder. Mix the fat and the milk up smooth, then add the other things, including some extra flour if it's too sticky. Then bake in a hot oven till just browned. They may not be the best to look at, but they are wonderful!"

"Reminds me of a squaw I knowed..." He looked quickly down at his plate. Grace turned red and got up to take some plates.

She brought out pie and coffee and the men thrilled with the skill of this woman. Skerby, especially, complimented her skills and his reward was an extra piece of pie. He grinned.

"You boys oughta learn from this!"

They all laughed as they watched Skerby plow through his pie.

Luke looked at the man. "Do you live in the mountains?"

Skerby paused. "No. I just like to wander around." He glanced at Teague. "I been doin' some special wanderin' fer a reason."

Teague squinted. "What do you need to tell me, Skerby?"

"I know where Barker is."

"Where?" Teague was suddenly tense. Grace looked over at him.

"Over the range to the west, at an old settlement up in the high country. He and that gun of his, Carson. I been trailing them and keepin' an eye on them. Looks like they're keepin' low till this blows over. I heerd them talkin' 'bout goin' back East. They're arguin' a lot, with that there Carson a mite testy about bein' up there with the snows comin' on. They're also talkin' 'bout finding gold."

Luke looked at Skerby with his mouth agape. "You been so close to them to hear 'em talk?"

Skerby chuckled. "Yup! Mite scarey to think someone might get that close, huh? Well, I ain't too rusty that I cain't do a mite of sneakin' now an' then." He winked at Luke.

"Can you guide me there, Skerby? Or tell me how to get there?"

"Sure, but they ain't gonna be goin' anyplace for a few days."

"I need to leave right away." Teague got up, grabbed his gun belt and flipped it around his waist as he limped out the door.

"He's awful eager."

"He jus' found out dat Barker was one of da men what kilt his wife an' son a few year back." Jinker stared at the door.

Skerby wiped his mouth as he pushed his chair back from the table. "My horse is tuckered out. You got one can carry a scrawny cuss like me?"

An hour later they rode out.

Chapter 23

"Where's all that gold you said we'd find, Barker." The man he was addressing did not miss the change of terms, from 'boss' to 'Barker' and the significance of the change.

He had created the story of the gold to keep the man content with being up in the high country. He had no real need for Carson, other than it was a mite more comfortable in this wild country with another man around. Also, he was not sure what he was going to do next and the extra hand might be handy. He had been able to keep paying Carson his wages from his money belt, but he had also noticed Carson eyeing his midsection where the belt rode underneath his heavy shirt. He knew decisions must be made soon and a course of action taken. Not only because of Carson, but because it was getting colder and they did not have winter gear with them. It was tolerable in the daytime, but night was a struggle to keep the fire going to ward off the chill. They had taken residence in the old log building, but it was mediocre at best with one wall partly collapsed and the sky showing through. They had not had rain, but the wind sure worked its way through. They had done some minor patching, but did not plan to stay long enough to worry about more.

"We must be off on the location. I know it's here. Let's go look again in that shaft up the hill. I think there was another tunnel we walked by."

Carson looked at the man as he followed. He had promised gold, but they had yet to find anything significant. A couple small nuggets and some dust, but nothing to keep them even through the winter. He was irritated. He had been fine the first week, but then he began to get the impression that this was just some sort of ruse, that there was never any gold. He was growing more interested in Barker's money belt. He could hear it clinking now and then, and Barker was very cautious about it. Must be a nice pile in there, he thought.

Barker was aware of the man's straying thoughts, having seen the glances and guessed the man's frustration. As they went into the tunnel, he was aware that Carson lingered a few paces further back, perhaps out of fear of what he, Barker, might do? Or perhaps planning something of his own?

"Here it is." Holding the candle, Barker bent and pointed. "See, our tracks bypass this tunnel."

As they proceeded down the tunnel, Barker began to wonder. This tunnel seemed like a strange off shoot. Suddenly he stopped. Carson almost ran into him.

"What the..."

"Back up, Carson." They backed and then Barker stooped closer to the ground and picked something up. He held it to the candle. Gold! It was a decent sized nugget. Both men's eyes grew large and they stooped again and both looked. Carson suddenly picked up another rock and turned it around. He took his pistol out, startling Barker, and bashed the rock with the butt, then held up another nugget. The men looked at each other.

"We're on to something, Carson. Let's see if we find more."

As happens when gold is involved, there was an instant increase in the suspicion each man had for the other. Gold changed friends to enemies as greed took over. If two men were already wary of each other, the addition of gold to the equation could lead to disaster. Both men knew this and both felt this, and they began to walk differently. They kept each other, or their light, more directly in sight.

As they came to a turn in the tunnel, they saw that it had not been cleaned out like most of the others, that there was fresh fall, likely from a blast. They slowed and came side by side. Both held their candles out in front.

Ahead and to their feet were two skeletons, half covered with rock. Apparently, these men had been too close to a blast, or a blast caused an unexpected cave in.

Carson spoke up. "I spent some time in the tunnels. Always hated it." He squinted ahead. "Looks to me like they had a short fuse, didn't get enough time to get away."

The two men walked carefully a few yards ahead, picking their way over rubble. Holding their candles out in front, both suddenly stopped and their gasps were audible.

There, within arm's length, was a large vein of gold, extending across the entire face of the tunnel.

"A fortune!"

"Carson, I suggest we split fifty-fifty. We're going to have to work together on this."

Barker knew the ramifications of this discovery. He could retire in style under a new name and live the high life. He also knew that greed had taken hold, and he had no intention of sharing this discovery with anybody. He also knew that Carson would have the same thoughts. It would be a fine act of manipulation, and both would be watching for opportunity to knock. Only one man could walk away with this. But at this point they needed each other to bring the gold out. Barker began to ponder.

Carson had the same thoughts. He knew that he must watch Barker like a hawk from now on. He also knew that neither man could share, that only one of them would get out with this gold. Besides, they only had two horses and one horse would be needed for carrying gold. One less body meant more gold a horse could tolerate.

They both turned, making deliberate effort to not look at each other, for fear of a conflict here and now, or that they might each see it in the others' eyes.

"Might as well get started." Barker tried to sound casual.

"Yep, might as well."

Chapter 24

Grace leaned against the post and stared off into the distance, watching as Lem and Skerby headed off into the mountains. She imagined she could still see them even after they were well out of sight.

Luke came and stood beside her.

"Will he come back, Grace?"

"I hope so, Luke." Then they stood side by side for some minutes before Luke wandered off. Grace remained staring into the distance, her mind running in different directions.

Will he come back? What she really wanted to tell Luke was that there was a chance that he might come back – if he was alive to come back. There were two killers at the other end of the journey, two killers who would not think twice about shooting Lem down in cold blood. They both knew his reputation, so they would be forewarned. Carson might take a chance, as he was looking for the reputation. Barker, on the other hand, was smarter than that and so would do something else if given the chance. Of course, Lem might catch them totally unawares, but his sense of right would compel him to give the men an even chance.

Carson would die first, wanting the reputation, and Barker would let it happen so as to see if both of his problems might be eliminated. She had seen him work more than once.

Try as she might, she saw danger for Lem. She didn't know Skerby enough to know how he would factor in to the situation.

Lem was in danger. Her man was in danger. There! She'd said it! He was her man! She had never been in love before, never been faced with someone she cared for so deeply being in mortal danger.

She stared into the distance.

"Jinker!"

He came out of the bunkhouse and to the post to stand beside her.

"Yes'm?"

"I'm going after him."

"Missus?"

"He's in danger, Jinker. I need to follow him."

"Missus Grace, I ain't so sure 'bout dat. Teague knows what he be doing, an' it be best he not haf to worry 'bout you while he's doin' what he be doin.'"

"I don't intend for him to know. I want to hang back far enough that he doesn't know I'm there and then I'll be there if he needs me. I have this bad feeling about those two men he's going to be up against. Barker is ruthless and Carson is a killer and both will be desperate."

"Missus…"

"I'm going, Jinker. I've got to. Maybe you don't fully understand, but I've got to go."

"Missus Grace, I guess I does understan' and I'se goin' wit' ya."

"Jinker, you aren't fully healed yet."

"Missus, usin' yo words, mebbe yo don' fully unnerstan' but I'se got to go. I'se got to make sho' yo get dere and I got's it to do."

An hour later she and Jinker rode out following Teague and Skerby. Grace had changed from her skirt into pants. Jinker rode stiffly, every now and then his hand going to his shoulder as he winced in pain. Grace followed him and noted his struggles.

Luke had been sent to town to find Kerner and stay with him and Emmy. He did so very reluctantly, arguing, but finally turning his horse and pouting off towards town.

Grace wanted to ride quickly but was keenly aware that she needed Jinker's tracking skills to keep on trail. He was unable to go faster due to his still-healing wounds.

She was so intent upon Jinker that she did not see the sudden dust plume in the distance as Luke turned his horse and filtered into the brush, following.

Miles down the trail, as that day began to fade, another set of eyes watched Grace and Jinker from a hillside. He was not seen because of his dusty, trail worn clothes and his care in remaining still. He was a man who had long been on the trail; a man who knew that movement was often what attracted the eye. So he sat his horse quietly, almost drowsily, weary himself from a long ride. Behind him was a packhorse, trail weary and glad for the break. From his vantage point, after watching the two riders, he let his eyes only shift to the distance behind Grace and Jinker, where he saw another rider, a child. He was hanging far back, yet the unknown rider wondered why the two in advance had not spotted him. He was almost undetectable, yet anyone with trail sense would have seen him.

Letting his eyes shift back to the two in front, he squinted his eyes in realization. One was hurt, slouching in the saddle. So he would be not attentive as usual to the back trail. It also was indicative that neither expected any trouble from the rear.

The man pondered the situation. The clues indicated that these riders were not outlaws, yet a man was wounded and they were riding into the mountains and not towards a town. One was a woman, and a child followed. His curiosity was piqued.

Waiting, immobile, until the young rider also passed, he slowly began his way down the slope. His trail would intersect with the riders ahead.

"We gots' to stop, Missus Grace. It's gettin' dark an' I gots' to get off'n dis hoss."

"Do you think we've kept up with them, Jinker?"

"I t'ink we's 'bout half day behin.'" His voice was strained, and he leaned more on his pommel. "Over dere, by dem trees and rocks."

When they reached the site, Grace quickly dismounted and hurried towards Jinker as he tried to dismount. She helped ease him down and held his arm as he lowered himself to a seat against a rock. Grace saw his shirt showing red where his wound was opened. She gasped as she saw it.

"I'se hurtin,' Missus Grace. I got's to take better care of dis wound an' bind it tighter for tomorrow." He grimaced. "I'se 'fraid you's gonna have to he'p an' take care of the cookin' an' such."

"I can do it all, Jinker. You just rest. I'll get some water boiling and we can see to that wound."

Jinker had his eyes closed and, gripping his shoulder with pain, nodded.

Grace quickly gathered sticks and started a fire, then put a small pot on to boil.

"Missus Grace?"

"Yes, Jinker?"

"Could you fetch me my rifle, please?"

"Why?"

"We got's comp'ny comin.'"

"What?"

"Dey's a man comin' to da camp. I seen him off towards da hills." She went to his horse and brought his Henry. He took it gingerly, putting the stock under his knee, while using his right hand to jack a shell in the chamber. He then placed the gun across his legs and waited.

"Go 'head an' git dinner ready. Jus' listen an' watch. Keep behin' da trees much as you can."

They didn't have long to wait.

"Hello the camp! Ok to ride in?"

"Come in witch ya hands careful!"

The man rode in, with his hands away from his guns. The man's mouth lifted on one side as he saw the wounded man with a Henry pointed across one leg. He'd never seen a man like this. He was a mulatto. Some may have questioned his parentage, but his abilities with a rifle were beyond question. The man was prepared.

"I saw you about an hour ago. Figured you might have coffee. I mean no harm."

"Light an' set, mister." The man noted that the rifle shifted to cover his moves as he dismounted.

"Mind if I reach into my vest pocket a moment?"

"I'se watchin.' Sorry mister, we jus' don' know who you is."

He raised both hands, reached into his vest pocket with his right hand and pulled out a silver sheriff's star. After buffing it on his shirt sleeve he slipped it in holes already in the left side of his vest.

"You's a sheriff?"

"Yes, though I have no jurisdiction here, I am a sheriff. I thought it might let you relax a mite. No need to keep that yellow boy pointed my way. I'm just a humble northern sheriff traveling through."

Jinker eased the hammer forward and visibly relaxed. The rider looked at Grace.

"Ma'am." He touched his hat brim.

"I'll have some coffee ready in a bit, Mr.?"

"Walt. Walt Larimore. I suspect the first water needs to be used to attend to a shoulder."

"No. We needs da coffee. I kin wait a bit."

"Mind if I take a look at that shoulder?"

"I reckon not."

Walt came over and knelt by Jinker. As he reached for the buttons, he spoke.

"You folks have names I can use?"

"I'se Jinker. Dis be Missus Grace."

"You can call me Grace."

He had Jinker's shirt open. Lifting the bandage, he looked thoughtful.

"The wound is healing, but this riding has broken it partly open. You've lost some blood. You've been healing a while, but not long enough for the wound." Looking over at Grace, he watched as she unpacked ham and put it in a pan.

"You folks obviously have not been out long, judging by the food." He grinned. "Not bad for trail food. But you need to cook more."

Both looked at him as he rose and stretched.

"There's another rider coming behind you. Been following you for some time. It's a kid."

"Luke!"

"You know him?"

"He's my brother, and he was to be heading to town."

"Well, you might as well invite him in. He somehow got off track and he's about a hundred yards yonder by those trees."

Grace looked into the fading light.

"Luke! Luke! We know you're there! Come on in!"

In just a few moments they heard him coming. He sheepishly came up to the fire.

"Luke, what are you doing? Why did you follow us?"

"I want to help Lem, too."

Grace threw her hands up and glared as she shook her head.

"Luke, this is dangerous. I do not want you hurt."

"I'll stay out of the way, Grace."

She stared at her brother.

"Guess I better put more ham on. Luke, go tie your horse with the others. Make sure you rub him down." The boy led his horse to the trees.

"Mister Larimore? What you doin' out here?"

"I'm headed back home, up Colorado way. Helped on a cattle drive and the other hands decided to head to California. I'm working my way back north. Little place called New Haven. That's where I'm the sheriff, if they haven't replaced me! I was told by a friend to look up a man named Grizzard to look at some cattle he's been breeding."

"Grizzard is my grandfather."

Chapter 25

The ride to the settlement took three days. Teague was quiet, brooding. Skerby would glance over at him now and then, wondering what must be going through his mind. It was on the second day that he got frustrated with the silence.

"Ya know, so little bein' said I might's well be goin' on this little jaunt by myself."

Silence.

"I recollect the time I was in the mountains fer six months by myself an' got to discussin' things wit' my mule and that jus' ain't right. Like to seen 'ol Bessie like she was human. Well, this here trip beginin' to feel the same way. Like mebbe I need to start talkin' to this horse to get any kind of decent conversation."

Silence.

"Ya know, Teague, we got's to be ready. We needs to have a plan. I come wit' ya to he'p, but ya got's to open yer mouth or I'se gonna go nuts!"

Silence, then Skerby was about to shake his head in defeat.

"She was beautiful."

"Who?"

"My wife. She was the most beautiful woman. She was the perfect wife for a preacher. A wonderful hostess, an exceptional mother too…" His shoulders began to wrack with sobs and he pulled his horse to a stop. The tears and grief began to roll off him. Never in all the years had the grief hit him so completely. Instead, he had held the feelings in, focused upon the mission of finding the killers. Now, with the end in sight, he could hold it no longer. He slid from his saddle and leaned against Rex, his shoulders continuing to heave with pent up pain. He began to grimace and shout with anger as he clutched the saddle horn with one hand and his face with the other.

Skerby sat and watched, wide-eyed, never having seen such grief shown by a man in the West. He was embarrassed, thinking a man should be able to be alone at such a time. He kept his gaze on the horizon, on the ridges, anywhere else, casting an occasional quick glance at the man known as hard and brave and willing to face the gates of Hell. A sobbing mass of humanity in front of him.

Finally, Teague quieted, but remained spent, leaning against Rex for some time. He looked at the saddle in front of him, wiping the tears off the leather with the flat of his hand.

"Four years ago my wife and son were killed in a robbery in St. Louis. They were just there, depositing money we were saving for a trip to Philadelphia to see her parents. The men came in and it...went wrong. Someone must've gotten jumpy and the town was alerted and as the robbers went out the back door they shot my wife and son and two others. Speculation was that someone's mask fell off and they killed the witnesses. To be that important, the mask must've been on the man in charge. I killed the other two, and neither was a leader, just a follower. So this man Barker must be the man who ordered them to be shot...likely shot them himself."

"Lord have mercy! I ain't never heard such a thing. You been searchin' all this time?"

Teague continued to look at the saddle. "Yes, but the trail went cold after I found the other two. Neither of them knew where the third had gone nor what his name was. As I tried to recreate the trail, I realized it was gone. I've just wandered around, hoping to find...oh, I don't know what I was hoping to find. A miracle perhaps."

"In the process of seeking the men, I gained a reputation as a man who was fast and deadly with a gun. Granted, even I realize that I am exceptionally fast and accurate, but I never intended to get a reputation. Now I can't get away from it."

Skerby dared to speak. "Well, sometimes God gives us a chance to start over. I know that you's on the way to do what's got to be done, but just mebbe they's a new start after this."

"Maybe." They both looked off into the distance. Finally Skerby spoke matter-of-factly. "If'n we's gonna find a place to camp fer the night, we gotta get off this hillside."

Teague mounted and they rode on, silent.

Carson and Barker worked side by side for two days, picking and grubbing at the gold vein. They got a good amount pretty well cleaned out and both men were extremely careful to avoid giving the other an opportunity to pull something. Another half day and they were wary but almost giddy, as in the process of working, Carson hit a lick and a pure nugget the size of a small billiard ball fell to the bottom of the shaft. Both were planning their futures with this sudden wealth, and both were planning with themselves alone. During meals and times of rest they acted very social, but that was on the surface. Barely underneath the surface, both were planning, conniving, plotting.

All thoughts of West Platte, lately known as Barkersville, were forgotten as the extent of the new opportunity took hold. Both were men of opportunity, prone to move from one glimmer of hope to another.

Carson was feigning sleep one evening while looking through squinted eyes and he saw Barker glance his way. The man picked up Carson's canteen and started to remove the lid. Snorting and gasping, Carson pretended to be waking, and Barker quickly put the canteen down.

What was he doing? He must be trying to poison me, Carson thought. He must be very careful from now until…

What he didn't know was that Barker was fully aware that he was pretending to be asleep. He deliberately faked the attempt to poison Carson in order to get his mind focused upon expecting that method. Barker, the man who watched others and found their weaknesses, knew that Carson was only able to think of one method to take out another man – by outdrawing and outgunning. It was a weakness, limiting his creativity.

Barker smiled inside.

Carson was, indeed, limited in his skills at planning. Nevertheless, he was also very fast with a draw. Yet he also had a weakness in that he was so intent upon being fast that he was not as careful to make the first shot count. Barker had seen more than once how Carson had beaten men to the draw. He had also noticed Carson's first shot went into the dirt and it was the second that killed the man. It was only his speed at the draw that allowed the two shots. And he had seen Carson practicing his speed when he thought Barker wasn't looking.

Barker had smiled inside then also.

And so the two men, allies, yet now mortal enemies, worked on, building wealth for one man, and that man yet to be determined.

Chapter 26

Soon after dinner, Jinker was asleep, his wound dressed. Grace had wiped the pan out and set is aside for the night. Walt smiled inside with the realization that she must be planning to cook something in the morning. That didn't always happen, with many camps eating only once a day and maybe chewing on some old jerky in the morning.

The coffee was good, too. Obviously this young lady knew what she was doing.

The sounds of the night were all around. Insects making their nighttime sounds and in the distance the hoot of an owl. The horses could be heard chewing contentedly on the grasses beyond the camp. Walt had shown Luke how to hobble the horses so they didn't stray too far. The boy was now nodding with weariness and would soon be out for the night.

Walt looked at Grace. She was seated against a rock and looked much into the darkness, as if looking or waiting for something.

"Expecting someone else, ma'am?"

"No. It's just that this has been a trying time, and the man – my man – is ahead of us and he is heading into danger." With that, she found herself telling this stranger of all the happenings of the past months and weeks. Larimore sat nursing this coffee.

"So your man – Lem – is heading after this man, this Barker and his hired gun. And you have headed after him, believing that he is in danger and that you must be there to help him."

"I guess that's what I'm thinking."

Larimore pursed his lips, raised his eyebrows and nodded as he brought his cup to his lips.

"Preacher. Ride a monster of a horse? Has a Circle-H brand?"

"Yes. How did you know?"

"He's kin to some friends of mine, back in Colorado. I met him when they gave him the horse. Circle-H is the Henry brand. He was on the trail of the killers of his wife and son. The piece of the story you didn't mention is that this Barker must be one of the killers of his wife and son?"

"Yes, there were three and he's found the other two. He feels this is the man who pulled the trigger."

"The Henry's are fine people, and treat me like family. I guess any kin of theirs are kin of mine."

Grace's eyebrows raised in a silent question.

Walt slugged the last of his coffee and stood up. "It's going to be slow going with a wounded man and a small boy. I don't expect Jinker will consent to being left behind, and Luke is too small to send packing back to town from this distance. That means we'll have to make an early start tomorrow, so we'd better get some sleep. My horses are half wild and will alert us if someone shows in the night.

It wasn't until she heard his slight snore that she realized what he'd said.

Teague and Skerby crawled up the backside of the small ridge above the old settlement, hats off. They raised their heads just enough to see over. The mountains were minor ranges, but folded and random, like a blanket given a shake and then laid down. The upper reaches of the ridges were rock, but where the settlement lay was in the bottom of the folds where there was the transition between scant foliage and the rocks above. There were scattered trees, stunted with the elements and gripping to whatever cracks they could find to hold a root. Indeed, some of the roots themselves had rent the rocks upon which they had sought a hold.

What Teague saw was a settlement, or a town or whatever such a cluster of old ruins would be called. It was a place that once barely existed. Built in a narrow cut through the mountain, the buildings were all contained in a quarter-mile caterpillar of shacks that never were improved because nobody stayed. From the remains it was obvious how quickly they had been built. Curled and warped boards lay pulled away from others by the unseen forces of the elements. Even now they could feel the wind blowing though the cut and whipping by their heads.

There were a couple shacks off on narrow tables of rock for those who got there first. The buildings were almost completely collapsed, the decades of neglect and abandonment having had their effect. Weathered gray boards turned to black and green with the onset of rot. The narrow road down the middle was barely wide enough for two wagons abreast and was overgrown with scrub and weeds. It was a forlorn place, a place of lost dreams and lost lives.

"This place have a name?" Teague asked Skerby in a whisper, as sound seemed to carry further in such a lonely place.

"Ain't got a name as I recall. Tweren't here long enough to get one."

They were silent for a few minutes as they quietly observed everything, watching or waiting for some sign of Barker and Carson.

"I expect we'll see some smoke before too long if they are still around. They'll be getting hungry and settling in."

"Unless they's digging in some shaft. Night an' day don' make no never mind underground. Course, if'n they are here, then it means we cain't have a fire anywhere's close."

"We'll have to camp cold tonight."

""I'se gonna miss my bacon an' coffee." Skerby frowned as they scooted backwards below the brow of the hill.

As they scooted further down the slope and rose to their knees, the wind brought a sound that brought them to a halt, their ears cocked back towards the town. It was the sound of a voice!

Barker and Carson were here.

Skerby looked at Teague and raised his eyebrows knowingly.

"Best wait'll the morrow, Teague. We can git a better idee of what's going on an' where's best to meet 'em."

Lem Teague looked at the man, then raised his eyes towards Heaven briefly, nodded and went to his horse.

Barker was a man used to having others do his bidding, preferring to sit back and watch others do the physical work. Yet, even he could not resist this lure of wealth. Gold fever, it was called. Even moral men turned scoundrel when caught by its vicious emotional tentacles. To men of already immoral character, such as Barker and Carson, it became an even deeper sickness of the mind, intertwining with the very soul and leading them straight to the pits of Hell.

Barker knew that only one of them would leave with the gold, and he intended it to be him, yet he still stashed the occasional nugget in his pocket instead of putting it in the sack they were filling. He knew Carson was doing the same, as he had cast a furtive glance at the man and saw his hand move away from his coat pocket…and that side of his coat seemed to sag a bit.

The men continued to hammer the ore apart and chip and use whatever they could to separate gold from what was mostly quartz. They had amassed several sacks and had them stashed.

And each man, indeed, had their own private collection of nuggets, which they had hidden under their saddles. Though each thought themselves unseen in their furtiveness, they both knew what the other was doing. Such was the way with men of their ilk. There was no trust but that given falsely by both, and both knew it. It was the sort of dream world in which the criminal mind lived, thinking they were more important or superior and needed, yet knowing inside they were but a pawn.

Carson knew of being a pawn. He just felt he was a better pawn, and that his gun skills made him more valuable. They did in a sense, but only as long as the skills served a purpose.

When the skills were no longer needed, neither was the man and all superficial friendship meant nothing after that point.

Barker could not conceive of being a pawn himself. He saw himself as a king, growing accustomed to others working to protect him because of his importance. His mind believed that his planning was better than anyone else's, leaving him blind to others schemes.

He didn't believe that Carson had a plan for him that would succeed. After all, the man was merely a gun hand, a paid gun.

Both men carried conversation as they worked, talking of this and that and all the nothingness in between.

Yet each continued to plan. And the pile of bits and pieces of fortune grew.

That night they rested against their saddles, their fire fueled with the wooden dreams of yesterday. They lay and cast furtive glances at each other, paranoid at this point, sure the other would act at any moment. Both had strewn rocks around their bedding, so as to create noise if someone approached. Each did so carefully, knowing it was being done but neither speaking of it for fear of causing the confrontation they each knew was coming. Sleep was fitful and disjointed.

Deep in the night, as Carson knew Barker was pretending to be asleep, he crept away and went to a dark corner and pretended to be hiding something. He knew Barker would be curious. Creeping back to his blankets, he smiled inside and actually slept.

Barker had seen every move. Carson had something hidden! It must be gold. He smiled inside. It would all be his.

Skerby grunted as he reached under his blanket and removed a rock he had missed.

"It ain't as easy to sleep on this hard ground as it once was. A body get's old an' wants somethin' soft. Don't get me wrong, I can still take it, but I sure appreciate when I get a chance at a bed. Happens two-three times a year. Then I find I can't sleep the first night 'cause I'm missin' the rocks! It just don't figure."

Teague smiled, then turned his head away.

Skerby was nervous, knowing that in the night he would be awakened by the man's nightmares. The night before, on the track of Barker, he hardly got any sleep.

If Skerby had seen Teague's eyes, he'd have seen the tears running in the darkness.

"How far are we, Mr. Larimore?"

"Never been there before, Grace, but from the looks of the tracks we'll catch up tomorrow morning. Maybe a couple hours behind them, if they stopped at dark. But I suspect things are going to be heating up."

"Can we go a bit further?"

215

Walt looked back at the other two riders, Jinker and Luke both slumped in the saddle. Jinker had done well enough, but he was pale and needing true rest. Dozing in the saddle was common, but it wasn't the same as lying down in complete rest.

Grace saw his glances and saw the same thing. Her eyes glanced ahead, boring into the darkness as if by looking hard enough she might see Lem. Walt glanced at her and then into the gathering darkness.

"I expect this is as far as we go. We got a couple really needing rest." Lowering his voice to a whisper, he said, "Jinker is in bad shape. Too much rough riding and he could go downhill. He's ok so far, but he is weary. Long ride for a man been hurt like he was."

Grace nodded and then went over to help Luke out of the saddle while Walt eased Jinker to the ground. The man was beat, but game.

"Tank ya kindly, sheriff. I'se a mite tuckered t'night."

"Much pain?"

"Not too bad, really. I'se jus' about as tired as I ever was."

"Just set tight while I lay out your blankets. Rest will be the best medicine. We'll get some dinner together."

Chapter 27

Two men arose, tense and glancing at each other as they quickly tore pieces off yesterday's rabbit and downed coffee. They each flinched involuntarily as the other grabbed metal tools, deep inside expecting this to be the moment of decision. Both were wrong.

Two others chewed cold jerky and biscuits, left their horses and began to work their way to the settlement.

Four others got a slower start, then mounted and began their journey.

The day would not be as any of them planned.

"This vein's about played out, Barker."

"I bet there's more if we get a bit more off the face."

The two men had worked for a half day and had not filled even a quarter of the sack. There was a pause and the tension was thick as coal dust.

"I dunno. Might be this is it." Carson's hand edged a mite closer to his gun. This tight tunnel would be a bad place to play with bullets, he thought.

Barker tensed, ready for a quick blow with the steel rod he held.

"How much we got?"

"I 'spect twenty pounds. Lotta money."

"That should keep a man living high for a long while."

"Guess we better get out of this tunnel."

"Yup. Go 'head. I'll follow."

"Naw, that's ok, we'll just walk out together. I'll take the bag."

Barker tightened his grip on the bar and subtly eased his arm back. For both it was an effort, as they each held a candle as well as Carson carrying a bag of ore and Barker the steel pry bar. Attacking the other would not be easy.

As the tension built to the breaking point, both men heard the sound at the same time. Sliding rock! It came from somewhere just outside the tunnel mouth. They had passed the place many times.

Someone, or somebody, was there! Suddenly, the uneasy alliance was reinstated by circumstance. Both men crouched and tilted their heads towards the tunnel mouth in the distance, hands on their pistol grips. Carson, the pawn, looked at Barker, the king, who gestured at him. Carson obeyed hesitantly and stepped forward, easing his foot down as he placed it carefully.

Teague and Skerby had come into the settlement from the east, and scouted carefully to try and locate Barker and Carson. Moving as quietly as their skills allowed, they finally located the men's gear in the only log cabin in the place, half broken down. Looking around, they saw tracks leading out of the cabin. The trail was well worn.

The men looked at each other, carefully checking their weapons. Each took one side of the street and then converged as the trail went between two ruins and up the mountainside.

The men pulled their pistols and started up the mountain. Muscles tensed, Teague led the way, knowing that at each turn the noise of their approach would be sensed by anyone there. Minutes later they came to a bend and saw the tunnel entrance. The tracks led in and there were two coats on a rock beside the trail. An empty sack lay on the ground.

Barker and Carson must be in the tunnel, Teague thought as he looked silently at Skerby.

Unspoken words passed between them. They looked at one another, as they both seemed to hear distant voices in the shaft. Walking forward to the entrance of the tunnel, guns drawn, they came to some shale. Stepping down carefully, Skerby nonetheless found the rock sliding under his foot and reached out to stay himself. The rock shifted noisily as Teague grabbed the man and stopped his fall.

Both men shrunk to the side of the tunnel entrance. No sound came from the tunnel. Surprise was now out of the question!

Not far away, yet approaching from a different angle than the others, Walt and Grace carefully worked their way around to find a vantage point over the settlement. Walking through some trees, they heard a horse nicker. Walt motioned for Grace to stop as he drew his gun and moved forward. It was a camp. He motioned Grace forward and she confirmed the items belonged to Teague and Skerby. Rex looked at them from some bushes.

Walt's eyebrows arched. "Land sakes! Never can get over the size of that horse!"

"Lem and Skerby must be up there looking for Barker. Let's follow!"

"Grace, one of the worst things you can do is follow. Right now he and Skerby face a known enemy. There is no one else. He can expect that anybody who shows is the enemy.

His decisions and reflexes are focused and ready. If we go working our way in, he will either shoot at us or, if he finds out you are here, have to stop and think before he responds to any threat. It could get him killed."

"So what am I supposed to do? I came here to help him."

"What we do right now is just...wait."

Carson slowly worked his way up the tunnel. It was perhaps 100 feet beyond where they had been when he was able to see the light of day around the curve. Carefully edging around, he was able to peer with one eye around at the entrance. He saw movement. He waited, then saw a face.

Preacher! His eyes glinted. He began to focus his every aim on this one prize. The gold lost its central point in his mind. Gone were the glimmers of riches and the dreams of women and power. Preacher!

His lust for superiority took over, and he knew he must do this thing. It drew him as from the core of his being.

He looked back down the tunnel where, in the distant darkness and curves, Barker waited for him. Barker, the wretch! He didn't need to worry about Barker. Barker could wait. He needed to kill this man known as Preacher! It was as if his whole life had built up to this chance for triumph.

Afterwards he would kill Barker and take the gold…

Chapter 28

Luke had never been good at waiting. Like all boys his age, he was curious and easily excited with new things. He wandered the campsite and poked around in the bushes for over an hour before he noticed Jinker was dozing.

Grace and Walt had gone up the trail a ways to see if they could see anything, leaving Jinker to watch the camp and look after Luke.

Jinker was tired. The wound and the riding had taken a deep toll. He tried his best to stay awake, but finally dozed after telling the boy to stay in the camp.

Then there was the rabbit.

Luke first saw the movement out of the corner of his eye. It was a mottled, dusky colored rabbit, a bit mangy looking. It did not seem too afraid, but turned and hopped a few steps between a couple bushes. Luke smiled and stepped slowly after it. When he was a few yards away it moved another few hops along what seemed a dim trail.

What a nice rabbit. As with all rabbits and the placement of their eyes, it seemed to be looking right at him. He smiled and, casting a quick glance at the sleeping Jinker, stepped after the rabbit.

It jumped around a bend in the trail and Luke scooted along after it. There it was! It moved again and he followed, over and over until he was out of sight of the camp.

What a skinny rabbit! He'd almost catch up to it and then the rabbit would move further. Luke laughed as he enjoyed the game.

Suddenly, rounding another bend, he spotted a small structure clinging to the hillside. It was gray and weathered and stood next to a pile of loose rocks strewn down the hillside.

He forgot about the rabbit and went to explore.

Barker hissed up the tunnel.

"Carson!" It'd been too long. He had no idea what had become of the man, except that he had somehow slipped out.

The gold! That was it! Carson had slipped out. The whole thing had been a ruse. Carson had rigged some rocks to fall! He had gone up the tunnel and was even now gathering up the gold and planning to take all the horses and leave him stranded up here on the mountain! Or was he up the tunnel waiting for Barker to come to where he could see him in the mouth of the tunnel? That would be it! Carson would wait till he came out of the tunnel and shoot him while he was blinded by the bright light.

He would fool Carson. The man did not know that when they had first explored this mine Barker had done some exploring on his own. Going by what appeared to be just a short shaft off the main tunnel, Barker had felt air. He had taken his candle and briefly strayed down and felt more air. It must be another tunnel to the outside. He had said nothing.

Now, if he could get past the Y in the tunnel without encountering Carson, then he could get out through that other tunnel and work his way back and hopefully arrive before Carson expected. He could grab the gold and both horses and be gone. Carson would never catch up without a horse. He felt his pocket for his extra candle. With a determined look unseen in the dark, he moved up the tunnel.

"We should not go any further, Grace." Walt glanced uneasily back towards the camp, then to the trail before them.

"I need to help him."

"You'll help him best by staying out of the way. We've got to see how this plays out before we go traipsing in."

They sat down on a large rock and waited. They weren't sure what they were waiting for, but they just…waited.

"I appreciate you helping us, Walt. You must be real eager to get back to your family, and here you've gone and gotten involved in someone else's troubles."

"Life has a way of throwing things at you. You take them as best you can and you do what you think best at the time. Yes, this wasn't exactly what I had planned, but it was the right thing to do. If the Henry's were here, they'd stick by their kin."

Suddenly they both shifted their glances up the trail as they heard distant gunshots.

A few minutes earlier, Teague and Skerby had backed away from the tunnel entrance as they had heard the sound of rocks being displaced in the tunnel. They drew back and watched as a man became visible as the light of the outside caught first his feet and worked upwards as he walked into the sunlight beyond the mouth of the cave. The face remained in the shadows of the hat, but the stance and the ways of the man gave him away.

Carson!

The gunman had slowly exited the tunnel, knowing instinctively as such men do that Teague would not shoot without giving him an even chance. Every man that Preacher was known to have killed was faced fairly. He couldn't say the same about himself. In fact, even now he would take any opportunity that came his way. Not that he needed it, for he knew he was faster.

As he came out of the tunnel, he waited for his eyes to adjust to the bright sunlight. He reached for his tobacco pouch as he spoke in a casual tone.

"Teague? Preacher?"

From around the up thrust of the rock, Preacher appeared. He was no longer Lemuel Teague for the moment, but purely Preacher. His senses keen, he knew that this was a showdown, that only one man would be alive in a few moments. Skerby watched from the other side of the trail over the rocks.

Carson chuckled as he rolled a smoke and put the sack into his shirt pocket, the tag hanging down.

"Well, Preacher, this is it. I knew when I first saw you that we would have to meet like this."

"Where's Barker?"

"Back down the tunnel, cowering."

"You can drop the gun, Carson, and you'll get out of this alive."

Carson chuckled again. "You know I can't do that."

"You're pretty confident."

"I killed Lew Holzer and Dandy Brooks."

"You've got that look in your eye, Carson."

'Yup."

I've seen it before – it's the look of a man about to die."

"I think that I will not bury you, Preacher. I think I will just leave you to the weather – and the wolves." He struck a match and lit his cigarette, but continued to hold the match in his hand. Preacher noticed this and smiled inside.

"I'll give you a decent burial, Carson. Even a dog deserves some dirt thrown over his carcass."

Carson chuckled again and then felt the heat of the match touch his fingertips. Acting startled, he cried out and at the same time went for his gun. The keen look in his eyes changed to triumph as both guns went off almost as one.

Preacher felt the blow as the bullet hit the ground at his feet and saw the incredulous look in Carson's eyes as he was sitting on the ground, looking down at his shirt. The tobacco tag was gone, and where it had been hanging, blood was oozing out of his chest.

Carson was watching the blood surge with each fainting beat of his heart. He looked down and saw the gun in his hand. He wanted to lift it but didn't seem to have the strength. He tilted his head and looked at Preacher. His mouth opened as if to say something, but his eyes suddenly looked empty and he fell back, dead.

Skerby came out from the rocks.

"I ain't never seen two men so fast! You hit?"

"No. His bullet plowed the dirt."

"I seen him holding the match."

"Yep, an old trick. Get his opponent to watch the match and lose focus on the man."

"No offense, but I'm glad he was a'gunnin' fer you and not fer me. I'da been kilt."

"He'll kill no more. Hard to tell how many righteous men he's killed just for pride. But the Good Book says that Pride goeth before a fall. He fell for sure." He flipped his cylinder out and reloaded. Somber, yet determined, he replaced the gun in the holster and looked towards the tunnel.

Barker.

Chapter 29

Still in the tunnel, Barker saw daylight as he headed downwards behind the cut of the mountain. Moments ago he'd heard distant shots and knew that something was amiss. Carson had run into something, or someone. That put a bit of the unknown back in the picture. Still, if he could just work his way back to the cache of gold, he could get out and start a new life and a new name. He'd done that before and had found himself recently trying out new first names, trying to find one that he would like being called. He had found himself liking Rafe, thinking that it sounded intelligent, yet sharp enough to sound like the name of a dangerous man. He liked being seen as a man not to hassle.

He stepped out of the tunnel and found himself in a small, wooden shack just big enough to give some protection as his eyes adjusted.

He heard movement and reached to his gun as he peered through a crack towards a trail along the side of the mountain.

That Gruber boy! What was his name? Luke. Yes, that was it. What was he doing here? It must mean his sister was here also. She had messed up his plans. He had a comfortable future here and she had slipped through his hands. He wanted her to suffer, and then die!

The boy was coming closer, heading for the shack. Barker crouched inside the door.

As Luke was about to enter, he reached out his hands to grab the boy and knocked a loose board, causing the boy to look up and see him. He had to step out and grab him as he turned to run. He missed, but grabbed a handful of the boy's jacket.

Luke screamed.

Grace and Walt had been looking upward towards the gunshots when they heard a distant scream. They both recognized it as Luke and began to run down the trail to the camp. They came to a stop in the camp. Jinker was nowhere in sight and they saw the marks of his boots down the other trail to the back of the mountain. They went quickly, but carefully, Grace in a panic. As they came around a bend in the trail they saw Jinker, shotgun in hand and the other hand clasped to his wound, facing someone they could not yet see. They knew Jinker wanted to look to see who it was coming behind him, but he was intent upon what was in front.

"Mister, you ain't gonna git way with dis. Let de boy go."

"Not hardly. Drop your gun or I will kill Luke!"

"Mister, you kill dat boy an' you'se a dead man."

Grace recognized the voice as Barker and lipped his name to Walt. Walt nodded and was about to step out to stand beside Jinker when a shot rang out and Jinker fell to the ground, grabbing at his leg. He rolled in agony as Walt leaped out, gun in hand, and faced the trail, only to find Barker squatted down behind Luke. There was no way to shoot without hitting the boy.

Barker yelled.

"Stay back or this kid will suffer!"

"Don't hurt the boy, Barker."

"You just stay where you are, mister." He backed into the shack and disappeared up the tunnel, carrying Luke!

Walt turned to Jinker, keeping an eye on the tunnel.

"How bad is it, Jinker?"

"Bleedin' pert bad, Sheriff. But I kin takes care of it. You go after dat boy!"

"Grace, stay with Jinker. You'll need to stop the bleeding. I'm headed back up to the settlement! You guard this end of the tunnel. If he comes back, you two will need to handle it."

Grace stood, caught between her desire to follow and the realization that Jinker needed help. She was in a near panic over Luke as she knelt by the man and tore off a piece of her shirt tail for a tourniquet.

Jinker noticed her hurried glances up the trail.

"Missus Grace, you got's to go help Teague. Take da shotgun an' go!"

"Are you sure, Jinker?"

"I be fine. Go!"

Lem Teague had heard the gunshot in the distance and ran back down the trail toward their camp, leaving Skerby at the cave mouth. He hit the camp just as another man he didn't recognize came in from the other direction. Instantly his gun was in his hand and the other man stood with hands in the air.

"Who are you?" Teague demanded.

"Name's Walt Larimore. I'm a sheriff from way up north. A friend of Bill Henry. I met you at their ranch when they gave you your horse. I been helping Grace find you. Barker's got Luke, headed up into a tunnel from below."

Teague's mind raced with questions, but the issue was at hand and questions needed to wait.

233

"It must come out up above. He was up there a while ago. Who's down below?"

"Jinker and Grace. Jinker's been shot."

"Bad?"

"He'll live."

"Is Grace ok?"

"She's fine."

"Watch Grace and Jinker and that end of the tunnel."

"Will do."

Teague turned and headed quickly to the settlement.

Barker heard the sound of boots on the loose rock as he came out of the tunnel mouth. Slipping sideways, he gripped Luke's mouth tight and cut behind the rocks towards the town. Luke squirmed and struggled and Barker stopped for a moment and held Luke at arm's length. He knocked him hard with his hand. The boy collapsed, unconscious, and Barker grabbed him and carried him under his arm. Looking back at the mouth of the cave he saw Skerby. Skerby reached for his gun.

Barker yelled. "Back off! Or I'll kill the kid!"

Skerby backed away.

"Drop the gun and turn around, hands behind you!"

When Skerby turned, expecting to feel his hands being tied, Barker slammed the gun barrel to his head. Skerby collapsed.

Hurrying, Barker worked his way to the ruins of the settlement and to the log structure where he and Carson had stayed.

Leaving the boy on the ground, he went around the wall and saddled his horse and Carson's, then led them by the fallen wall of the cabin and began to quickly tie on the gold sacks.

Pity, he thought, to leave the other sack in the tunnel. But he couldn't go back for it. These sacks must have forty or fifty thousand in them. More than enough. Grabbing a canteen by the fire, he started to climb into the saddle when he thought of the other night when Carson went to the far corner in the night. Gold! Carson had a stash! A little bit more.

Lowering himself, he went to the back where he found a rumpled blanket Carson had apparently placed over his stash. Picking up the blanket, he saw fresh dirt where a hole had been dug and covered with a board. He grinned as he bent over to lift the board but his look turned to shock as the coiled rattlesnake struck, biting him in the side of his face. Barker cried out, fell and scrambled backwards as the snake hung from his cheek, caught. Barker finally flung the snake away.

He grabbed his face, cursing Carson. The man had set a trap for him!

235

Teague heard the cry down the street and began to run, finally slowing and stepping carefully around the corner of the building. He saw Barker grabbing at his face and cursing. He guessed what had happened.

Barker sensed Teague's presence and grabbed Luke off the ground, spinning amazingly quick to place the child in front of him as a shield. Luke was awake again, staring wide-eyed.

"Back off, Preacher! Back off or I will kill this boy!"

"Barker, you're a dead man."

"I ain't dead yet! Men been known to live from snake bite."

"I can see the teeth marks. It got you good, lot's of poison." This was the man who had taken all that was worth anything away from him! He stared a deep, dark look at Barker.

"Why did you follow me here, Preacher?"

"You killed my wife and son in a robbery in St. Louis. You took my life away from me! I've been looking for you ever since." His face was red with fury.

Dawning realization shown on Barker's face.

"Does this boy mean anything to you?" Barker sneered.

"Let him go!"

"Preacher, if you don't drop your guns now I will kill this boy. I swear it!" He was almost screaming. "If it is as you say and I am a dead man, then you must realize I have nothing to lose." He jammed the gun barrel cruelly into Luke's cheek, pointed towards the top of his head. He had a look in his eyes that even Teague knew as the wild eyes of a deadly man. "Drop them! I will give you five seconds and I will not ask again."

Teague, in a fury but still realistic, set his guns to the ground. He had no options. Barker grinned through the pain and looked at Teague with triumph. He dropped Luke and stood, extending the gun towards the man known as Preacher.

He laughed. It was the laugh of a crazy man. "I remember well that robbery. I had to kill them. They were witnesses. But now I'm going to kill you and you can join them."

Teague felt the bullet as he turned with the impact and stumbled to his knees. Grasping his side, he felt the blood and reached for his Baby Patterson behind his hip. He spun and shot as Barker's next shot hit the dirt in front of him. Squinting from the dust, he saw Barker stumble, grasping a shoulder with one hand. He was on his knees, with Luke, terrified, on the ground in front.

"You got no reason to live now, either, Preacher." Barker's finger tensed on the trigger

237

as his mind heard a sound to his left. He had no time to look.

Suddenly Barker was jolted as Luke kicked him and scooted away. Barker flung himself to the side, behind the cover of a large boulder. His gun was instantly trained upon Teague, who had moved closer.

"I will kill you, then the boy, before I die!"

The sound of a cocking hammer startled him, and he looked to his left and saw Grace. He started to shift his gun. Preacher fired and Barker lurched. He looked and saw Grace, turning his gun to her, a pained leer on his face as his life dripped from him.

She held the revolving shotgun level and fired, tearing Barker in two as he fired, his bullet wild. His body flopped against the wall, lifeless.

Preacher stood, staring... He looked from what was left of Barker to Grace. She heard him sigh heavily, and saw his shoulders sag. She went to him. He reached out. They held close, both sagging with the weariness of deep and long-held tension.

Tension that was no more.

Two weeks later, Jinker hobbled out of the bunkhouse, weak but healing, to stare at the colorful sunrise. Lem motioned him over to a seat and grimaced as he stood to shake his friend's hand. Both grinned at each other.

Jinker winced. "I 'spect ain't much work been done round here with the men all stove up."

"I heard that nonsense, Jinker Jackson!" It was Grace's voice from the kitchen. Moments later she came out with steaming cups of coffee for each of them.

"Do you hear any bawling cattle? Do you see any corral boards loose? Have you missed a meal? Did you make the coffee? Let me tell you, mister, that even with you laying around eating free food all the work has been getting done! Luke and I have been handling it, along with a couple of my grandfather's men."

Jinker glanced at Lem, who just grinned ear to ear back at him. But Grace was not finished.

"Hired hands around here need to pull their weight. I think since you are able to drink my coffee, you are quite well enough to get to work patching some harness. Before lunch." Catching Lem's grin, she addressed herself to him. "And you...when you are done with your coffee, you can get in the house and do the dishes. There's not a blessed thing wrong with your hands."

Grace turned and went back in the house. Jinker leaned back in his chair. He and Lem looked at each other and grinned.

"She got's what it takes to run dis place, ain't she?"

"Yep. And she's friends with Rex. He even let her ride. Never happened before."

239

Jinker nodded knowingly and they sat a few moments. He shifted in his seat, straightening his leg.

"Walt headed t'home?"

"Yep, headed out couple days ago. Grizzard gave him some cows and one of his prime bulls to take back to Colorado. Sent a couple men along to help." Jinker nodded his approval.

"I hear tell the town done elected a mayor?"

"Kerner, the bartender. He married Emmy Sunday."

"You don't say!" They both grinned again.

"I think the town will do well now."

"Yessir, dey's a lot less 'citement an' we ain't got to be on edge so much."

"A bit more relaxed than the last time we sat down together, my friend."

"Skerby?"

"He's around somewhere. Been here for a couple meals. I hear Grizzard sent word that he'd like to talk when he comes to town next week."

"Never know where dat Skerby'll show up!"

"What're your plans, Jinker?"

"I like it here, Lem. Good food an' it feel good to be treated like a man." He leaned forward and cast a sideways look at the window. He smiled knowingly at his friend. "They's a nice lookin' woman cooks at the hotel. She come by to see me t'other day. Purty little thing. Brung me a apple pie! Yep, things is good.

Missus Grace says I gots a home here if'n I want it." He leaned back in his chair and sighed.

They both paused a few moments. There were the pleasing sounds of Grace preparing breakfast, and the wafting smells of the frying bacon.

Jinker looked over to Teague and spoke quietly. "What'cha gonna do, Lem?"

There was another pause and the sounds in the kitchen ceased. Both men glanced at the nearby window. Grace had keen ears.

It was Lem's turn to sigh, from deep within. He looked around at the ranch and the mountains basking in the orange glow of the morning. He felt a deep peace, a happiness, and a long lost sense of home. He looked at Jinker and the kitchen window. He spoke to the window.

"I think my life starts over again right here."

The clinking of the dishes began again, accompanied by the happy humming of a smiling young woman.

About the Author

Mark Herbkersman spent his high school and college years in Idaho. He holds a B.A. in History from Boise State University and a Master's in Counseling Psychology from Ball State University. He has been a Counselor, a seminar presenter/speaker, adjunct faculty at Butler University, a pastor, and now an author.

An avid reader all his life, Mark grew to love the adventure and clear morals of the classic western authors, with his favorite being Louis L'Amour.

He resides in Indiana with his wife, Marilyn, and their two daughters.

Check out his blog at markherb.blogspot.com. , or email at askmherb@yahoo.com He will gladly respond to your comments!